THE HALFWAY HOUSE

Guillermo Rosales

THE HALFWAY HOUSE

INTRODUCTION BY JOSÉ MANUEL PRIETO
TRANSLATED BY ANNA KUSHNER

A NEW DIRECTIONS PAPERBOOK ORIGINAL

Manufactured in the United States of America
Published simultaneously in Canada by Penguin Books Canada, Ltd.
New Directions Books are printed on acid-free paper.
First published as a New Directions Paperbook (NDP1144) in 2009

Library of Congress Cataloging-in-Publication Data

Rosales, Guillermo.
  [Casa de los náufragos. English]
  The halfway house / Guillermo Rosales ; introduction by José Manuel
Prieto ; translated by Anna Kushner.
    p. cm.
  ISBN 978-0-8112-1802-3 (pbk. : alk. paper)
  1. Halfway houses—Florida—Fiction. 2. Exiles—Florida—Fiction.
3. Cubans—Florida—Fiction. 4. Psychological fiction. I. Kushner, Anna. II. Title.
  PQ7390.R665C3713 2009
  863'.64—dc22

                                                                2009005947

New Directions Books are published for James Laughlin
by New Directions Publishing Corporation,
80 Eighth Avenue, New York 10011

CONTENTS

Introduction by José Manuel Prieto   1

The Halfway House   13

INTRODUCTION
BY JOSÉ MANUEL PRIETO

It's not difficult to see a parallel between the life Cuban writer Guillermo Rosales (Havana, 1946-Miami, 1993) led in the United States as an outsider to the American experience and the imagined existence of his alter ego William Figueras in a halfway house or "Boarding Home" as those came to be known in Miami. Rosales, a lifelong misfit who was diagnosed early on with severe schizophrenia, went into exile in 1979 with a history of mental illness. It wasn't long before he descended to the only spot available to him, "one of those marginal refuges where the desperate and hopeless go."

The time he spent in several of these institutions provided Rosales with the material to write the novel you have in your hands. The work itself, its powerful condemnation of the Dantean existence of the wards' miserable existence under the complicit watch of deceitful managers, must be read in the light of his experiences. Rosales wished to unveil the existence of these infernos, writing about the many halfway houses allowed to operate so cruelly thanks to the indifference of a community focused on achieving the American dream, of refugees from Castro's regime who may have continued to ponder their painful expulsion from Cuba but were determined to get ahead at all costs.

The novel's halfway house is not, however, the efficient jail-like institution (representative of the oppressive state) that appears in Ken Kesey's *One Flew Over the Cuckoo's Nest*, a place governed by cleanliness and order. Rosales' description of the "boarding home" is full of murky similes: toilets that are always "clogged with old shirts, sheets, curtains," flooded again and again with "feces, paper and other filth"; the color of Arsenio's skin, Curbelo's sinister Lieutenant, is "dirty as puddle water," while the eye of one of the nuts, Reyes, is oozing constantly. The place is a sort of sewer where misfits end up and are preyed upon by Curbelo, the manager, whose main hobby, not coincidentally, is deep-sea fishing.

People from all walks of life have ended up in this sinister place, this circle of Hell: Ida, "the grande dame come to ruin"; René and Pepe, "mental retards" whose fights Figueras watches with indifference; Hilda, the decrepit old hag sexually abused by Arsenio; Eddy, a nut who lost everything in Cuba and who demands that the United States use an atomic bomb to wipe out all the communists in the world. Cubans aren't the only residents; there's Louie, the American, who swears and curses all the time, and Napoleon, the Colombian, a four-foot tall midget, "fat and solid," Rosales says with his incredible precision, "as a speed bag."

In contrast to the other residents, Figueras is an educated man: "I, William Figueras who read all of Proust when I was fifteen years old, Joyce, Miller, Sartre, Hemingway, F. Scott Fitzgerald, Albee, Ionesco, Beckett...," Rosales, himself impressively well-read, also endows his alter ego with rich intellectual baggage. Figueras will be the one, with his strong narrative voice, to firmly drive the story without stumbling for a single moment, without ever falling into the nonsensical talk of the demented.

Just one detail stands out about him: he is a dejected man who arrives at the halfway house beaten down by History. "They thought a future winner was coming, a future businessman, a future playboy... The person who turned up at the airport... was a crazy, nearly toothless, skinny, frightened guy..." In essence, and this is important to understanding the book, Figueras is a survivor, yet someone who can't manage to make a life for himself outside of Cuba. He is someone who has escaped the overwhelming totalitarian experience, but for whom the damage persists. Figueras shares that curse of conscience described by Sophie in William Styron's *Sophie's Choice*, "My purity was an inward-dwelling Golgotha," as well as that burden carried by the "damaged" characters in Isaac Bashevis Singer's novel *Enemies, A Love Story*.

This explains his passivity, his inability to adapt to his new country, his having gone as low as the halfway house without offering any resistance. But what makes this character truly complex is that Figueras is not only a victim but also a victimizer. What it deals with—and Rosales understands this very well, his character's ambiguity is his greatest achievement—is the absolutely most destructive way in which the Totalitarian State makes you complicit in its cruelty and terror. At the end of the passage I cited above, the one beginning with "I, William Figueras who read all of Proust when I was fifteen years old ...," he adds: "I who lived twenty years within the revolution, as its *victimizer, witness, victim*." (The italics are mine.)

Herein lies the depth of Figueras' tragedy. Beyond acting as a condemnation of the halfway house, of Miami, or of the inhumane capitalism that makes no room for losers like him, Rosales decisively moves the origins of his character's story to the past, to the time just before going into exile.

Hence the importance of his dreams, the retelling of seven prophetic dreams that appear in this book. In them, Figueras examines entire areas of his life in Cuba that bloom in his dreams as images and revelations. In the novel, the function of these visions is to carry Rosales' explorations beyond the murky present of the halfway house, revealing the substrata where the damage took place. Thus, in the first dream Figueras describes a ghost town, an image that is later expanded on in the fifth dream in which he wanders around a Havana in ruins. In his second dream, he is tied to a rock, now a character with "nails ... long and yellow like a fakir's." A sort of bound Prometheus who nonetheless is surrounded by octopi that he tyrannizes sadistically, "the octopi shed large crystalline tears at my cruelty." He is tied to a rock but he tyrannizes them to the point of tears, forcing them to find him treasures that he immediately casts away with a diabolical laugh. He then dreams that he is shooting at a house in which Fidel Castro (who is also a character in the novel, although he only appears in dreams), "as agile as a mountain lion," dodges his shots. Fidel Castro and all that he represents is Figueras' deeply embedded past, difficult to remove, indestructible. In the second to last dream, Fidel has died but his coffin opens up, he steps out, and asks for a cup of coffee: "Well, we're already dead," Fidel said: "Now you'll see that doesn't solve anything, either." The damage inflicted, Rosales wants to tell us, runs so deep that it will persist even beyond death.

In another revealing passage, Figueras is watching *el Puma*, a famous Latin American singer, on television and he can't establish a clear difference between *el Puma*'s life, a rather apolitical one, if you will, and his own, with the burden he bears. *El Puma* is someone who lives painlessly, superficially one could say, because: "He will never desperately embrace an ideology only to feel betrayed by it. He'll never feel his heart go 'crack' in the face of an idea in which he firmly and desperately believed. Nor will he know who Lunacharsky, Bulganin, Kamenev or Zinoviev are. He'll never feel the joy of taking part in a revolution or the subsequent anguish of being devoured by it. He'll never know what the machinery is. He'll never know."

It's worth pointing out that this is the same difference existing between the other inhabitants of the halfway house, real mentally insane people, and the image that the narrator has of himself. At no point in the more than one hundred pages of this book does the author signal any truly serious problem, "medical" or "mental," in his character. In other words, I hold a radically different view from the reading of this novel as simply autobiographical, according to which our protagonist would be someone like Rosales himself, with severe mental problems. The distinction is important because it points to the fact that the other inhabitants have ended up at the "Boarding Home" blamelessly, or *as if they were blameless*. They are truly demented. Only Figueras, who knows himself to be guilty, paradoxically, has full use of his reason. The others are pure victims, for lack of a better term.

Figueras knows he is guilty (always in the sense previously pointed out, that of someone who took an active and enthusiastic part in the inevitable cruelty of the revolution), but hasn't found redemption. He joins "mafia" forces with Arsenio and at one point towards the middle of the book, he comes to recognize: "I've gone from being a witness to being complicit in what happens in the halfway house." Every once in a while, he is visited by his friend, *el Negro*, a poet with whom he discusses literature, and in his free time, pierced by desire, he flips through pornographic magazines: the author wants to tell us that his character is not entirely dead.

And then Frances appears: "There's a new crazy woman sitting in front of the set. She must be my age. Her body, while cheated by life, still has some curves." She is a woman who is still young, but more importantly, "the new crazy woman" has not lost her humanity and Figueras perceives this instantly. The revelation of this detail in the book is masterly: the woman trembles when Figueras approaches her for the first time and inspects her unscrupulously. Frances, like himself, is completely conscious of the halfway house's sordidness. She's not "crazy," rather, she's "shipwrecked" like Figueras, and he feels immediately attracted to her.

Figueras goes back and forth between tenderness and cruelty. On two occasions, he starts to strangle the woman to the point of asphyxiation, making her black out. Frances offers no resistance to the torture because she confesses herself broken, "dead inside," and is the only one who, like him, understands her own guilt, the terrible duality of her condition. And this shared guilt is the basis for their understanding each other.

During their first walk around Little Havana, already as a couple, they talk about it. "My angel," Frances asks him, "were you ever a communist?" "Yes," Figueras responds. "Me too," Frances affirms. And in the scene that immediately follows—heart-rending because of its profound meaning and its symbolic location inside the "big, gray" arcade of a Baptist church—both of them chant an anthem "from the early years of the Revolution." The two seem to be saying, yes, we had a past in the Revolution, we believed in it, we chanted anthems and slogans, we were part of its terrible machinery.

It's surprising that this moment has gone unremarked by almost all critics. We stand before what can be considered the book's neurological center. Everything stems from here, its importance, its very genesis. Because once the guilt is understood, they turn to art to redeem themselves, to leave testimony of the past.

Which is what makes this book great, imbuing it with deep human significance. Rosales, like no other Cuban author before him, knew how to leave behind the narrow road of victimhood for the larger, more arduous one of full responsibility. He looked deep into the tragedy and found himself to be part of it. This is his truth, the important discovery that the book brings to us: we are all responsible, all of us, in one way or another we took part in it, were small pieces, no matter if unconsciously so, of that great oppressive machine. He must, then, communicate his discovery, put it into words. Hence the importance of literature for his character, the conversations he holds about his literary idols: Hemingway, Truman Capote. Hence the fact that Figueras arrives at the asylum with a book of English poets: literature is the tool for the great task he sees before him, that of leaving a truthful and blunt testimony of the Hell that is the halfway house, but above all, and most significantly, of his past as part of the great machinery.

Yet one obstacle presents itself: the experience of that existence within "history," within the nature of the totalitarian phenomenon, is of such utter otherness that it ends up being virtually untranslatable. It's a recurring complaint in the literature written by exiles, survivors of totalitarianism. The problem appears in Milan Kundera, Joseph Brodsky, in Alexander Solzhenitsyn himself. It's an impediment that makes them feel they cannot be saved. "Nobody understands," Frances confesses at another key moment of the book upon speaking of the years lived in Cuba, during the euphoria of the Revolution: "I tell my psychiatrist and he just gives me strong Etrafon pills."

It thus requires the talent of a great writer to articulate this, the tenacity of an artist who views this task as the great goal of his life, although he proclaims himself beaten from the very beginning: "The house said 'Boarding Home' on the outside, but I knew that it would be my tomb." Once there, however, he will fight to leave his mark; he knows he is lost, but he will leave his testimony. To his endless surprise, Figueras discovers that Frances is also an artist. She draws and does it so well that he is amazed when she shows him the drawings she has been making of the asylum's inhabitants: "It's done in the style of primitive artists. It's very good . . . , Everything is exact. It also breathes its own life . . . She's really good! She has captured all of our souls." Exactly the feat of the memoirs of Primo Levi (another suicide like Rosales), exactly the feat of Varlam Shalamov's powerful *Kolyma Tales,* and of every artist survivor. In art the unnamable tragedy acquires a voice and is vanquished. The artist fights to leave his mark, knows he is lost, but will allow the victims to speak in his book.

Which is how the novel closes with such majestic force—the moment in which the possibility of conquering fate scintillates: the couple makes plans, they opt for believing in a miracle to get them out of there. Figueras imagines himself living with Frances like a normal man: "If she weighed a few more pounds and took better care of herself, she'd be pretty." He feels so certain of success that during the walk he takes, once he and Frances have agreed to leave the halfway house, he fraternizes with unknown people in the streets and, to his great luck, runs into a neighbor from his childhood in Cuba. Figueras knows he is saved and the tone of the story changes: "As I pass by Pepe . . . I take his bald head in my hands and kiss it . . . I burst out laughing."

Finally, the dream of escape is dashed, but it's no longer entirely tragic for Figueras. Not only did he find love, he also found a person like himself who was purified by repentance, who has achieved moral re-grounding.

Very little is known about how an unknown author like Guillermo Rosales came to be the writer of excellence who appears here, the possessor of a unique style and the author of what is, without a doubt, one of the best Cuban books of the second half of the twentieth century, comparable only to the mythical Carlos Montenegro's *Men Without Women* or Reinaldo Arenas' famous memoir *Before Night Falls* (adapted for film by Julian Schnabel in 2001). Although Rosales practiced journalism in Cuba and always considered himself a writer, between the year of his arrival in Miami and the fateful morning of his suicide, there was very little in the public eye that stood out in terms of literature. While still in Cuba, Rosales had had a brush with fame or perhaps the hope of better luck for his work with *El juego de la Viola,* a novel which was a 1968 finalist in the prestigious "Casa de las Américas" contest. He did participate, along with the now internationally known Reinaldo Arenas, in one of the most interesting cultural project of the 1980s, the *Revista Mariel* (1983–1985). In it, Rosales published the only interview he gave while alive and in which, besides discussing his double exile—from Miami's petit bourgeois and from revolutionary Cuba—he makes a very revealing clarification about his characters that confirms the reading I propose here and that places the condemnation of the ravages of totalitarianism as the central theme of this novel. His characters, Rosales says, "are Cubans affected by Castro's totalitarianism, human wrecks."

At some point in 1987 his friend, the writer Carlos Victoria, sent the manuscript for *The Halfway House* to the prestigious *Letras de Oro* (Golden Letters) contest, sponsored by American Express and with Octavio Paz, the Mexican future Nobel laureate, on the jury. Thanks to its obvious structural qualities and the cataclysmic power of the story, the book ended up winning. Nonetheless, nothing happened: the book had a lukewarm reception among Spanish-language critics and for years was known only by a few people.

In 2002, the French edition published by Actes Sud with the title *Mon Ange (My Angel)* was a resounding success. The newspaper *Le Monde* praised it as "a spectacular autobiographical fable" as well as a "lyrical and lapidary" novel. The following year, it was reissued in Spain under the title *La Casa de los Náufragos (The House of the Shipwrecked)* to great acclaim.

In 1993, the time of his death, Guillermo Rosales was forty-seven years old.

THE HALFWAY HOUSE

THE HOUSE SAID "BOARDING HOME" on the outside, but I knew that it would be my tomb. It was one of those marginal refuges where the desperate and hopeless go—crazy ones for the most part, with a smattering of old people abandoned by their families to die of loneliness so they won't screw up life for the winners.

"You'll be fine here," my aunt says, seated at the wheel of her straight-off-the-assembly-line Chevrolet. "You'll understand that nothing more can be done."

I understand. I'm almost grateful that she found me this hovel to live in so that I don't need to sleep on benches and in parks, covered in grime and dragging sacks of clothes around.

"Nothing more can be done."

I understand her. I've been admitted to more than three psychiatric wards since I've been here, in the city of Miami, where I arrived six months ago, fleeing the culture, music, literature, television, sporting events, history and philosophy of the island of Cuba. I'm not a political exile. I'm a complete exile. Sometimes I think that if I had been born in Brazil, Spain, Venezuela or Scandinavia, I would have also fled those streets, ports and meadows.

"You'll be fine here," my aunt says.

I look at her. She gives me a long, hard look. There's no pity in her dry eyes. We get out of the car. The house said "Boarding Home." It's one of those halfway houses that pick up the dregs of society. Beings with empty eyes, dry cheeks, toothless mouths, filthy bodies. I think such places exist only here, in the United States. They're also known simply as homes. They're not government-run. They're private houses that anyone can open as long as he gets a license from the state and completes a paramedic course.

". . . a business just like any other," my aunt explains to me. "A business like a funeral home, an optician's, a clothing store. You'll pay three hundred dollars here."

We opened the door. There they all were: René and Pepe, the two mentally retarded men; Hilda, the decrepit old hag who constantly wets herself; Pino, a gray, silent man who just glares at the horizon with a hard expression; Reyes, an old one-eyed man whose glass eye

ERM:

---

constantly oozes yellow liquid; Ida, the grande dame come to ruin; Louie, a strong American with greenish-yellow skin who constantly howls like a mad wolf; Pedro, an old Indian, perhaps Peruvian, silent witness to the world's evils; Tato, the homosexual; Napoleon, the midget; and Castaño, a ninety-year-old geezer who can only shout "I want to die! I want to die! I want to die!"

"You'll be fine here," my aunt says. "You'll be among Latinos."

We go on. Mr. Curbelo, the owner of the Home, is waiting for us at his desk. Did I find him repulsive from the very beginning? I don't know. He was fat and shapeless, and was wearing a ridiculous track suit made all the worse by a juvenile baseball cap.

"Is this the man?" He asks my aunt with a smile on his face.

"This is him," she responds.

"He'll be fine here," Curbelo says, "like he's living with family."

He looks at the book I'm carrying under my arm and asks, "Do you like to read?"

My aunt responds, "Not only that. He's a writer."

"Ah!" Curbelo says with mock surprise. "And what do you write?"

"Bullshit," I say softly.

Then Curbelo asks, "Did you bring his medicines?"

My aunt looks in her purse.

"Yes," she says. "Melleril. One hundred milli-grams. He has to take four a day."

"Good." Mr. Curbelo says with a satisfied face. "You can leave him then. We'll take care of everything else."

My aunt turns to look into my eyes. This time, I think I see the slightest trace of pity.

"You'll be fine here," she assures me. "Nothing more can be done."

My name is William Figueras, and by the age of fifteen I had read the great Proust, Hesse, Joyce, Miller, Mann. They were for me what saints are to a devout Christian. Twenty years ago, I finished writing a novel in Cuba that told a love story. It was the story of an affair between a communist and a member of the bourgeoisie, and ended with both of them committing suicide. The novel was never published and my love story was never known by the public at large. The government's literary specialists said my novel was morose, pornographic, and also irreverent, because it dealt harshly with the Communist Party. After that, I went crazy. I began to see devils on the walls, to hear voices that insulted me—and I stopped writing. All I produced was a rabid dog's froth. One day, thinking that a change of country would save me from madness, I left Cuba and arrived in this great American country. There were some relatives waiting for me here who didn't know anything about my life and who, after twenty years of separation, barely knew me anymore. They thought a future winner was coming, a future businessman, a future playboy, a future family man who would have a future house full of kids, and who would go to the beach on weekends and drive fine cars and wear brand-name clothing like *Jean Marc* and *Pierre Cardin*. The person who turned up at the airport the day of my arrival was instead a crazy, nearly toothless, skinny, frightened guy who had to be admitted to a psychiatric ward that very day because he eyed everyone in the family with suspicion and, instead of hugging and kissing them, insulted them. I know it was a great disappointment for everyone, especially for my aunt who was expecting something great. They got me instead. An embarrassment. A terrible mark on this fine Cuban petit bourgeois family with their healthy teeth and buffed fingernails, radiant skin, fashionable clothes, who were weighed down by thick gold chains and owned magnificent cars of the latest make and spacious houses with well-stocked pantries and central heat and air-conditioning. That day (the one on which I arrived), I know that they all eyed each other with embarrassment, made some scathing comments and drove off from the airport without any intention of ever seeing me again. And that's the way it's been. The only one who remained faithful to the family ties was this Aunt Clotilde, who decided to make herself responsible for me and kept me at her house for three months, until the day when, at the advice of other friends and relatives, she decided to stick me in the halfway house: the house of human garbage.

"Because you'll understand that nothing more can be done."

I understand her.

This halfway house was, originally, a six-room house. Perhaps it was once inhabited by one of those typical American families who fled Miami when the Cubans fleeing communism began to arrive. Now the halfway house has twelve tiny rooms, with two beds in each room. In addition, it has an ancient television set that's always broken, and a kind of living room with twenty folding chairs that are falling apart. There are three bathrooms, but one of these (the best one) is reserved for the boss, Mr. Curbelo. The toilets in the other two are always clogged since some of the residents stick in them old shirts, sheets, curtains and other cloth materials that they use to wipe their behinds. Mr. Curbelo does not give us toilet paper, although he is supposed to by law. There is a dining room, outside the house, tended by a Cuban *mulata* with scores of religious necklaces and bracelets whose name is Caridad. But she doesn't cook. If she were to cook, Mr. Curbelo would have to pay her an additional thirty dollars per week, and that's something Mr. Curbelo would never do. So Mr. Curbelo himself, with his bourgeois little face, is the one who makes the stew every day. He makes it in the simplest way, by taking a handful of peas or lentils and dropping them (plop!) in a pressure cooker. Maybe he adds a little garlic powder. The rest, rice and a main dish, comes from a home delivery service called "Sazón," whose owners, knowing they're dealing with a nut house, pick the worst they have and send it over any which way in two huge greasy pots. They should send enough food to feed twenty-three people, but they only send enough for eleven. Mr. Curbelo thinks this is enough and no one complains. But if a complaint does arise, then Mr. Curbelo, without even looking at the person, says, "You don't like it? Well if you don't like it, leave!" But . . . who's going to leave? Life on the streets is hard. Even for crazy people whose brains are on the moon. And Mr. Curbelo knows this and repeats, "Leave, quickly!" But nobody leaves. The complainer lowers his eyes, grabs his spoon and goes back to swallowing his raw lentils silently.

Because in the halfway house, no one has anyone. Old Ida has two kids in Massachusetts who want nothing to do with her. Quiet Pino is all alone and doesn't have anyone at all in this huge country. René and Pepe, the two mentally retarded guys, could never live with their weary relatives. Old one-eyed Reyes has a daughter in Newport that he hasn't seen in fifteen years. Hilda, the old lady with cystitis, doesn't even know her own last name. I have an aunt . . . but "nothing more can be done." Mr. Curbelo knows all of this. He knows it well. That's why he is so sure that no one will leave the halfway house and that he will continue to receive the checks for $314 that the American government sends for each one of the crazy people in his hospice. There are twenty-three nuts: $7,222. Plus, with another $3,000 that comes from I don't know what supplemental source, it comes to $10,222 a month. That's why Mr. Curbelo has a well-appointed house in Coral Gables and a farm with racehorses. That's why he spends his weekends perfecting the fine art of deep-sea fishing. That's why his kids' photos appear in the local paper on their birthdays, and he goes to society parties wearing tails and a bow tie. Now that my aunt is gone, his face, once warm, eyes me with cold indifference.

"Come along," he says dryly. He takes me down a narrow hallway to a room, number four, where another crazy guy is sleeping with a snore that reminds me of an electric saw.

"This is your bed," he says, without looking at me. "This is your towel," and he points at a threadbare towel full of yellowish stains. "This is your closet, and this is your soap," and he takes half a piece of white soap from his pocket and hands it to me. He doesn't say another word. He looks at his watch, realizes how late it is and leaves the room, closing the door behind him. Then I put my suitcase on the floor, place my small television set on top of the armoire, open the window wide and sit on the bed assigned to me with the book of English

poets in my hands. I open it at random, to a poem by
Coleridge:

> *God save thee, ancient mariner!*
> *From the fiends that plague thee thus!–*
> *"Why look'st thou so?" –With my cross bow*
> *I shot the Albatross.*

The door to the room suddenly opens and a robust figure, with skin as dirty as puddle water, comes in. He
has a can of beer in his hand and takes several sips from
it while giving me the once-over out of the corner of
his eye.

"You're the new guy?" he asks after a while.

"Yes."

"I'm Arsenio, the guy who takes care of things
when Curbelo leaves."

"Okay."

He looks at my suitcase, my books and stops at
my small black-and-white TV set.

"Does it work?"

"Yes."

"How much did it cost you?"

"Sixty dollars."

He takes another swig, without taking the corner of his eye off of my TV set. Then he says, "Are you
going to eat?"

"Yes."

"Then get going. The food's ready."

He turns around and leaves the room, still

drinking from his can. I'm not hungry, but I should eat. I only weigh 115 pounds, and I tend to get woozy. People on the street sometimes yell *"Worm!"* at me. I throw the book of English poets on the bed and button up my shirt. My pants swim around my waist. I should eat.

I head toward the dining room.

Miss Caridad, the one in charge of distributing food to the crazy people, points out the only open spot to me. It's a seat next to old one-eyed Reyes, and across from Hilda, the decrepit old hag whose clothes reek of urine, and Pepe, the older of the two mentally retarded men. They call this table "the untouchables' table," since no one wants to be with them when it's time to eat. Reyes eats with his hands, and his enormous glass eye, as big as a shark's eye, constantly oozes watery pus that falls down to his chin like a large yellow tear. Hilda also eats with her hands and does so reclined in her chair, like a marchioness eating delicacies, so that half of the food ends up on her clothes. Pepe, the retarded guy, eats with an enormous spoon that looks like a spade. He chews slowly and loudly with his toothless jaw, and his whole face, up to his large popping eyes, is full of peas and rice. I bring the first spoonful to my mouth and chew slowly. I chew once, three times, and then I realize that I can't swallow it. I spit everything out onto my plate and leave. When I get to my room, I notice that my TV set is missing. I look for it in my closet and under the bed, but it's not there. I go in search of Mr. Curbelo, but the person sitting at his desk now is Arsenio, the second in command. He takes a swig from his can of beer and informs me,

"Curbelo's not here. What's up?"

"My TV set has been stolen."

"Tsk, tsk, tsk," he moves his head in despair. "That was Louie," he then says. "He's the thief."

"Where's Louie?"

"In room number three."

I go to room number three and find Louie the American, who howls like a wolf when he sees me come in.

"TV?" I say.

"Go to hell!" He exclaims, furious. He howls again. He throws himself at me and pushes me out of the room. Then he shuts the door with a loud slam.

I look at Arsenio. He smiles. But he hides it quickly, covering his face with the beer can.

"A sip?" he asks, holding the can out to me.

"No thanks, I don't drink. When will Mr. Curbelo be in?"

"Tomorrow."

Great. Nothing more can be done. I go back to my room and let myself fall heavily on the bed. The pillow stinks of old sweat. The sweat of other nuts who have been through here and shriveled up between these four walls. I throw it far away from me. Tomorrow I'll ask for a clean sheet, a new pillow and a lock to put on the door so that no one enters without asking first. I look at the ceiling. It's a blue ceiling, peeling, overrun with tiny brown cockroaches. Great. This is the end of me, the lowest I could go. There's nothing else after this halfway house. Just the street and nothing more. The door opens again. It's Hilda, the decrepit old hag who urinates on her clothes. She has come in search of a cigarette. I give it to her. She looks at me with kind-hearted eyes. I notice a certain beauty of yesteryear behind that revolting face. She has an incredibly sweet voice. With it, she tells me her story. She has never married, she says. She's a virgin. She is, she says, eighteen years old. She's looking for a proper gentleman to marry. But a gentleman! Not just anyone.

"You have beautiful eyes," she says sweetly to me.

"Thank you."

"You're welcome."

I slept a little. I dreamt I was in a town in the provinces, back in Cuba, and that there wasn't a soul in the whole town. The doors and windows were wide open, and through them you could see iron beds with very clean, tightly pulled white sheets. The streets were long and silent, and all of the houses were wooden. I was running around that town in distress, looking for anyone to talk with. But there was no one. Only open houses, white beds and total silence. There wasn't a single hint of life.

I awoke bathed in sweat. In the bed next to me, the crazy guy who was snoring like a saw is awake now and putting on a pair of pants.

"I'm going to work," he tells me. "I work all

night at a pizza place and they pay me six dollars. They also give me pizza and Coca-Cola."

He puts on a shirt and slides into his shoes.

"I'm an old slave," he says. "I'm reincarnated. Before this life, I was a Jew who lived in the time of the Caesars."

He leaves with a slam of the door. I look at the street through the window. It must be midnight. I get up from the bed and go to the living room, to get some fresh air. As I pass Arsenio's room, the hospice manager, I hear bodies struggling and then the sound of a slap. I continue on my way and sit in a tattered arm chair that reeks of old sweat. I light a cigarette and throw my head back, fearfully remembering the dream I just had. Those white, tightly made beds, those wide open solitary houses, and I, the only living being in town. Then I see somebody coming out of Arsenio's room. It's Hilda, the decrepit old hag. She's naked. Arsenio comes out behind her. He's naked too. They haven't seen me.

"Come on," he says to Hilda in a drunk voice.

"No," she responds. "That hurts."

"Come on, I'll give you a cigarette." Arsenio says.

"No. It hurts!"

I take a drag of my cigarette and Arsenio discovers me among the shadows.

"Who's there?"

"Me."

"Who's me?"

"The new guy."

He mutters something, disgusted, and goes back inside his room. Hilda comes over to me. A ray of light from an electric street lamp bathes her naked body. It's a body full of flab and deep valleys.

"Do you have a cigarette?" she asks in a sweet voice.

I give it to her.

"I don't like getting it from behind," she says. "And that pig!" she points to Arsenio's room. "He only wants to do it that way."

She leaves.

I lean my head against the back of the arm-chair again. I think of Coleridge, the author of "Kubla Khan," whose disenchantment with the French Revolution provoked his ruin and sterility as a poet. But my thoughts are soon cut off. A long, terrifying howl shakes the boarding home. Louie, the American, shows up in the living room, his face bursting with rage.

"Fuck you up the ass!" He screams at the street, which is empty at this late hour. "Fuck you up the ass! Fuck you up the ass!"

He slams his fist against a mirror on the wall and it falls to the floor in pieces. Arsenio, the manager, says lazily from his bed,

"Louie, you *cama* now. You *pastilla* tomorrow. You *no jodas más*."

And Louie disappears into the shadows.

*　　*　　*

Arsenio is the real one in charge at the halfway house. Even though Mr. Curbelo comes every day (except Saturday and Sunday), he's only here for three hours and then he leaves. He makes the stew, prepares the day's pills, writes something or other in a thick notebook and then leaves. Arsenio is here twenty-four hours a day non-stop, without even a quick run out for cigarettes. When he needs a smoke, he asks one of the nuts to go out to the bodega for him. When he's hungry, he sends Pino, his peon, out to get him food at a joint on the corner. He also sends for beer, lots of beer, because Arsenio spends all day getting completely drunk. His friends call him Budweiser, the beer he drinks most. When he drinks, his eyes become more evil, his voice becomes even thicker, and his gestures ruder and cruder. Then he kicks one-eyed Reyes, he opens anyone's drawers in search of money and he walks around the entire boarding home with a sharpened knife at his waist. Sometimes, he takes this knife, gives it to René, the retard, and points at one-eyed Reyes, saying, "Stick it in him!" He further explains, "Stick it in his neck, it's the softest part." René, the retard, takes the knife with his clumsy hand and moves forward on the old one-eyed guy. Although he stabs blindly at him, he never wounds him, since he's not strong enough. Then Arsenio sits him down at the table; brings an empty beer can over, and plunges the knife into the can. "That's how you stab!" he explains to René—"like this, like this, like this!" and he stabs the can until he pierces it through. Then he puts the knife back in his belt, gives the old one-eyed guy a savage kick in the behind, and sits down at Mr. Curbelo's desk again to have another beer. "Hilda!" he calls out later. And Hilda, the decrepit old hag who stinks of urine, comes. Arsenio touches her sex through her clothes and says, "Wash yourself today!"

"Get away, will you!" Hilda complains, indignant. And Arsenio bursts out laughing. And his square and sweaty torso is slashed through with a scar that goes from his chest to his navel. It's from being stabbed in prison, five years ago, where he was doing time for stealing. Mr. Curbelo pays him seventy dollars a week. But Arsenio is happy. He has no family, no profession, no life ambitions, and here, in the halfway house, he's a big fish. For the first time in his life, Arsenio feels fulfilled somewhere. Besides, he knows that Curbelo will never fire him. "I am his everything," he goes around saying. "He'll never find another guy like me." And it's true. For seventy dollars a week, Curbelo will not find another secretary like Arsenio in the whole United States. He won't find him.

I woke up. I fell asleep in the tattered armchair and woke up around seven. I dreamt I was tied to a rock and that my nails were long and yellow like a fakir's. In my dream, although men tied me up as a punishment, I had great power over the world's animals. "Octopi!" I screamed, "bring me a shell engraved with the Statue of Liberty." And the large, cartilaginous octopi toiled with their tentacles to find that shell among the millions and millions of shells in the sea. Then they found it and struggled to bring it up to the rock where I was captive and they oh so humbly and respectfully handed it over to me. I looked at the shell, let out a peal of laughter, and threw it scornfully into the great void. The octopi all shed large crystalline tears at my cruelty. But I laughed at their weeping, and roared, "Bring me another one just like it!"

It's eight in the morning. Arsenio hasn't woken up yet to serve breakfast. The nuts huddle, starving, in the TV room.

"Senio!" Pepe the retard screams. "Rekfast! Rekfast! When you gonna serve rekfast?"

But Arsenio is still drunk and snoring belly-up in his room. One of the nuts turns on the TV. Out comes a preacher talking about God. He says he was in Jerusalem, that he saw the Garden of Gethsemane. Pictures of the places where he wandered appear on the screen. There's the River Jordan, whose clean, gentle waters are impossible to forget, the preacher says. "I've been there," says the preacher. "Two thousand years later, I've inhaled Jesus' presence." And the preacher cries. His voice becomes pained. "Hallelujah!" he says. One of the nuts changes the channel. This time he puts on the Latin channel. Now there's a Cuban commentator talking about international politics.

"The United States has to get tough," he says. "Communism has infiltrated our society. It's in the universities, the newspapers, the intelligentsia. We should go back to the great Eisenhower years."

"That's right!" says a nut next to me named Eddy. "The United States needs the balls to wipe them out! The first to go has to be Mexico, which is full of communists. Then Panama. And Nicaragua after that. And wherever there's a communist, string him up by the balls! The communists took everything from me. Everything!"

"What did they take from you, Eddy?" asks Ida, the grande dame come to ruin.

Eddy responds, "They took almost a thousand acres of land planted with mangos, sugarcane, coconuts . . . everything!"

"My husband had a hotel and six houses in Havana taken away from him," says Ida. "Oh! And three pharmacies and a sock factory and a restaurant."

"They're sons of bitches!" Eddy says. "That's why the United States has to wipe them out. Drop five or six atomic bombs! Wipe them out!"

Eddy starts shaking.

"Wipe them out!" he says. "Wipe them out!"

He shakes a lot. He shakes so much that he falls out of his chair and keeps shaking on the floor.

"Wipe them out!" he shouts from there.

Ida yells, "Arsenio! Eddy is having a fit!"

But Arsenio doesn't answer. Then Pino, the silent nut, goes to the sink and comes back with a glass of water that he throws over Eddy's head.

"Enough." Ida says. "Enough. Turn off that TV."

They turn it off. I get up. I go to the bathroom to urinate. The toilet is clogged with a sheet someone stuck inside. I urinate on the sheet. Then I wash my face with a bar of soap I find lying on the sink. I go to my room to dry myself off. The crazy guy who works nights at the pizza place is counting his money in our room.

"I earned six dollars." He says, putting his earnings away in a wallet. "They also gave me pizza and Coca-Cola."

"I'm glad," I say, drying myself off with a towel.

Then the door opens abruptly and there's Arsenio. He just woke up. His wiry hair is standing up and his eyes are bulging and dirty.

"Listen," he says to the lunatic, "gimme three dollars."

"Why?"

"Don't worry. I'll pay you back."

"You never pay me back," the lunatic complains in a childish voice. "You just take and take and never pay me back."

"Gimme three dollars," Arsenio repeats.

"No."

Arsenio goes over to him, takes him by the neck with one hand and goes through his pockets with his free hand. He finds the wallet. He takes four dollars out and throws the other two on the bed. Then he turns to me and says, "You can tell Curbelo about everything you see here, if you want. I'll bet ten to one that I win."

He leaves the room without closing the door and yells out from the hallway,

"Breakfast!"

The nuts come out in droves after him, toward the tables in the dining room.

Then the crazy guy who works at the pizza place grabs the two dollars he has left. He smiles and exclaims happily,

"Breakfast! Great! I was starving."

He leaves the room too. I finish drying off my face. I look at myself in the room's stained mirror. Fifteen years ago I was a good-looking guy. I was a lady-killer. I showed off my face arrogantly everywhere I went. Now . . . now . . .

I grab the book of English poets and go to breakfast.

Arsenio hands out breakfast. It's cold milk. The nuts complain that there are no cornflakes.

"Go tell Curbelo," Arsenio says indifferently. He grabs the milk bottle carelessly and starts filling the glasses with apathy. Half of the milk ends up on the floor. I grab my glass and, standing, gulp it down on the spot in one fell swoop. I leave the dining room. I reenter the main house and sit down in the tattered armchair again. But first I turn on the television. A famous singer comes on, a man they call *El Puma*. The women of Miami worship him. *El Puma* gyrates. "*Viva, viva,*

viva la liberación," he sings. The women in the audience go wild. They start throwing flowers at him. *El Puma* moves his hips some more. "*Viva, viva, viva la liberación*": *El Puma*, one of the men who makes the women of Miami tremble. The same women who won't even deign to look at me, and if they do it's only to tighten the hold on their purses and quicken their steps fearfully. I've got him here: *El Puma*. He has no idea who Joyce is, and doesn't care. He'll never read Coleridge, and doesn't need to. He will never study Marx's *Eighteenth Brumaire*. He will never desperately embrace an ideology only to feel betrayed by it. He'll never feel his heart go "crack" in the face of an idea in which he firmly and desperately believed. Nor will he know who Lunacharsky, Bulganin, Kamenev or Zinoviev are. He'll never feel the joy of taking part in a revolution or the subsequent anguish of being devoured by it. He'll never know what the machinery is. He'll never know.

All of a sudden, there's a big ruckus on the porch. Tables are knocked over, chairs crash, and the metallic walls shake as if a mad elephant were bashing into them. I run over. It's Pepe and René, the two retards, fighting over a slice of bread smeared with peanut butter. It's a prehistoric duel—a dinosaur fighting a mammoth. Pepe's arms, large and clumsy as octopus tentacles, beat blindly at René's body. The latter uses his nails, as long as a kestrel's claws, digging them into his adversary's face. They roll onto the floor in a bear hug, noses bleeding and frothing at the mouth. No one intervenes. Pino, the silent one, continues looking at the horizon without blinking. Hilda, the decrepit old hag, looks for cigarette butts on the floor. One-eyed Reyes sips a glass of water slowly, savoring every swallow as if it were a highball. Louie, the American, flips through a Jehovah's Witness magazine that discusses the paradise to come at the final hour. Arsenio watches the fight from the kitchen, smoking calmly. I go back to my seat. I open the book of English poets to a poem by Lord Byron:

> My days are in the yellow leaf;
> The flowers and fruits of love are gone;
> The worm, the canker, and the grief
> Are mine alone!

I don't read any further. I lean my head back in the armchair and close my eyes.

Mr. Curbelo arrived at ten in the morning in his small gray car. He was jovial. Caridad, the *mulata* who hands out the food to the nuts, praises how youthful and elegant he looks today to get in his good graces.

"I won a solid fourth place." Mr. Curbelo says.

Then he explains, "In deep-sea fishing. I won fourth place. I reeled two in that were forty pounds each."

"Oh!" Caridad the *mulata* smiles.

Mr. Curbelo enters the halfway house. All of the nuts immediately run up to ask him for cigarettes. Mr. Curbelo takes out a pack of Pall Malls and hands cigarettes out to the nuts. He doesn't look at any of them. He distributes the cigarettes quickly, impatiently, as irritated as Arsenio when he hands out the milk in the mornings. The nuts have their first smoke of the day. Mr. Curbelo buys a pack of cigarettes daily and hands them out each morning when he arrives. Because he's a good person? Not at all. According to federal law, Mr. Curbelo is supposed to give each nut thirty-eight dollars a month for cigarettes and other incidentals. But he doesn't. Instead, every day he buys a pack of cigarettes for everyone, so the nuts don't get too frantic. This is how Mr. Curbelo robs the nuts of over seven hundred dollars monthly. But even though they know all that, the nuts are incapable of demanding their money. It's tough on the streets . . .

"Mr. Curbelo," I say, approaching him.

"I can't see you right now," he says, opening the closet where the medicines are kept.

"I've had my television set stolen," I say.

He ignores me. He opens a drawer in the closet and takes out dozens of bottles of pills which he places on top of his desk. He looks for mine. Melleril, 100 milligrams. He takes one.

"Open your mouth," he says.

I do. He pops the pill in it.

"Swallow," he says.

Arsenio watches me swallow. He smiles. But when I look right at him, he hides the smile by drawing a cigarette to his mouth. I don't need to investigate any further. I know perfectly well that it was Arsenio himself who stole my television set. I understand that to complain to Curbelo is useless. The guilty party will never turn up. I turn on my heel and go toward the porch. I get there just as old one-eyed Reyes takes his small, wrinkled penis out and starts to urinate on the floor. Eddy, the nut who is well-versed in international politics, gets up from his seat, goes over to him, and delivers a brutal punch to his ribs.

"You're disgusting!" Eddy says. "One day I'm going to kill you."

The old one-eyed man moves back. He shakes, but doesn't stop urinating. Then, without putting his penis away, he falls into a chair and grabs a glass of water off the floor. He drinks, savoring the water as if it were a martini.

"Ah!" he exclaims, satisfied.

I leave the porch. I go out to the street, where the winners are. The street is full of big, fast cars with heavily tinted windows so that vagabonds like me can't snoop inside. I pass a café and hear someone call out to me,

"¡Loco!"

I turn quickly. But no one is looking at me. The customers are drinking their drinks, buying their cigarettes, reading their newspapers silently. I realize it's the voice I've been hearing for fifteen years. That damned voice that insults me relentlessly. That voice that comes from a place unknown but very close. The voice. I walk on. North? South? What does it matter? I continue. And as I continue on, I see my body reflected in the shop windows. My whole body. My ruined mouth. My cheap and dirty clothes. I continue. On one corner, there are two female Jehovah's Witnesses selling the magazine *Awaken*. They accost everyone, but let me pass without saying a word. The Kingdom was not made for down-and-out guys like me. I continue. Somebody laughs behind my back. Infuriated, I turn around. The laughter has nothing to do with me. It's an old lady praising a newborn. Oh, God! I start walking again. I get to a very long bridge over a river of murky water. I lean on the railing to rest. Winners' cars speed by. Some of them have the radio turned all the way up, blasting pulsating rock songs.

"You're going to tell *me* about rock and roll?" I scream at the cars. "Me! I who came to this country with a picture of Chuck Berry in my shirt pocket!"

I continue. I get to a place they call *downtown,* full of gray, slapdash buildings. Elegantly dressed Americans, black and white alike, leave their workplaces to eat a hot dog and drink Coca-Cola. I walk among them, ashamed of my threadbare checked shirt and of the old pants that dance around my hips. I end up going into a shop that sells pornographic magazines. I go over to the rack and pick one of them up. I feel my penis stiffening a little and I crouch on the floor to hide my erection. Oh, God! Women. Naked women in all the positions imaginable. Beautiful women belonging to millionaires. I shut the magazine and wait a minute for the excitement to pass. When it has passed, I stand up, put the magazine back and leave. I walk on. I walk on into the heart of downtown. Until I stop, tired, and realize it's time to go back to the halfway house.

I get to the halfway house and try to enter through the front door. It's locked. A maid, whose name is Josefina, cleans the house inside, so the nuts have been banished to the porch.

"Get out, *locos!*" Josefina says, pushing them all out with a broom. And the nuts leave without complaint, taking their seats on the porch. It's a dark porch, surrounded by black metallic cloth, with an ever-present puddle of urine at the center thanks to old one-eyed Reyes, who has lost all shame and urinates everywhere all the time, despite the punches he receives on his squalid chest and gray, unkempt head. I turn around and sit on one of the porch chairs, inhaling the strong smell of urine. I take the book of English poets out of my pocket. But I don't read any of it. I just look at the cover. It's a beautiful book. Thick. Finely bound. *El Negro* gave it to me when he came back from New York. It cost him twelve dollars. I look at some of the illustrations in the book. I see Samuel Coleridge's face again. I see John Keats, he who in 1817 asked himself,

> *Ah! why wilt thou affright a feeble soul?*
> *A poor, weak, palsy-stricken, churchyard thing,*
> *Whose passing-bell may ere the midnight toll*

Then Ida, the grande dame come to ruin, gets up from her chair and comes over to me.

"Do you read?" she asks.

"Occasionally," I respond.

"Oh!" She says. "I used to read a lot, back in Cuba. Romance novels."

"Oh!"

I look at her. She dresses relatively well compared to the way the other people at the halfway house dress. Her body, while old, is clean and smells vaguely of cologne water. She's one of the ones who knows how to exercise her rights and demands her thirty-eight dollars a month from Mr. Curbelo.

She was a member of the bourgeoisie back in Cuba, in the years when I was a young communist. Now the communist and the bourgeois woman are in the same place, the same spot history has assigned them: the halfway house.

I open the book of Romantic English poets and read a poem by William Blake:

> *Little Lamb, who made thee?*
> *Dost thou know who made thee,*

Gave thee life & bid thee feed
By the stream & o'er the mead

I close the book. Mr. Curbelo pokes his head through the porch door and motions to me with his hands. I go. At his desk, a well-dressed, well-groomed man is waiting for us with a thick gold chain around his neck and a large watch on his wrist. He's wearing a fetching pair of tinted glasses.

"This is the psychiatrist," Mr. Curbelo says. "Tell him everything that's the matter with you."

I take a seat in a chair that Curbelo brings me. The psychiatrist takes a piece of paper out of a folder and starts to fill it out with a fountain pen. While he writes, he asks me, "Let's see, William. What's the matter?"

I don't answer.

"What's the matter?" he asks again.

I take a deep breath. It's the same bullshit as always.

"I hear voices," I say.

"What else?"

"I see devils on the walls."

"Hmmm!" he says. "Do you talk to those devils?"

"No."

"What else do you have?"

"Fatigue."

"Hmmm!"

He writes for a long time. He writes, writes,

writes. He takes off the tinted glasses and looks at me. His eyes don't show the slightest interest in me.

"How old are you, William?"

"Thirty-eight."

"Hmmm!"

He looks at my clothes, my shoes.

"Do you know what day today is?"

"Today," I say uncomfortably. "Friday."

"Friday, the what?"

"Friday . . . the fourteenth."

"Of what month?"

"August."

He writes again. While he does, he discloses impersonally, "Today is Monday, the twenty-third of September."

He writes a little more.

"Okay, William. That will be all."

I stand up and go back to the porch. There's a surprise for me there. *El Negro* has come to see me all the way from Miami Beach. He has a book in his hand and he holds it out to me as a greeting. It's *Time of the Assassins* by Henry Miller.

"I'm afraid it will ruin you," he says.

"Stop fucking with me!" I reply.

I take him by the arm and lead him to a broken-down car that sits in the garage of the halfway house. It's a car from 1950 that belongs to Mr. Curbelo. One day it just stopped forever and Mr. Curbelo left it there, at the halfway house, so it would go on deteriorating, slowly, along with the nuts. We get in the car and sit in the back seat, between oxidized springs and pieces of dirty padding.

"What's new?" I anxiously ask *El Negro*. He's my link to society. He goes to meetings with Cuban intellectuals, talks about politics, reads the papers, watches television, and then, every week or two, he comes to see me to share the gist of his travels through the world.

"Everything's the same." *El Negro* says. "Everything's the same . . . ," he says. Then, all of a sudden: "Well! Truman Capote died."

"I know."

"That's it," *El Negro* says. He takes a newspaper out of his pocket and gives it to me. It's the *Mariel* newspaper, edited by young Cubans in exile.

"There's a poem of mine in there," *El Negro* says. "On page six."

I look for page six. There's a poem called "There's Always Light in the Devil's Eyes." It reminds me of Saint-John Perse. I tell him. He's flattered.

"It reminds me of *Rains*," I say.

"Me, too," *El Negro* says.

Then he looks at me. He takes in my clothes, my shoes, my dirty, tangled hair. He shakes his head disapprovingly.

"Hey, Willy," he then says, "you should take better care of yourself."

"Oh, am I that run down?"

"Not yet," he says. "But try not to get any worse."

"I'll take care of myself," I say.

El Negro pats my knee. I realize that he's about to leave. He takes out a half-empty pack of Marlboros and gives it to me. Then he takes out a dollar and gives that to me, too.

"It's all I have," he says.

"I know."

We get out of the car. A nut comes up to us to ask for a cigarette. *El Negro* gives him one.

"*Adios*, Doctor Zhivago," he says, smiling. He turns around and leaves.

I go back to the porch. As I am about to go in, somebody calls to me from the dining room. It's Arsenio, the halfway house second-in-command. He's shirtless and hiding a can of beer under the table since it's not right for the psychiatrist who's visiting the residence today to see him drinking.

"Come here," he says to me and points to a chair.

I go inside. Besides him and me, there's no one else in the dining room. He looks at the books I have in my hand and starts laughing.

"Listen . . . ," he says, drinking from the can. "I've been watching you closely."

"Yeah? And what do you make of me?"

"That you're not crazy," he says, still smiling.

"And what school of psychiatry did you go to?" I ask, irritated.

"None," he replies. "I just have street psychology. And I'll tell you again that you, you're not crazy! Let's see," he then says, "take this cigarette and burn your tongue."

I'm disgusted by his idiocy. His malt beer-colored body, the huge scar that goes from his chest down to his navel.

"You see?" he says, taking a swig of beer. "See how you're not crazy?"

And then he smiles with his mouth full of rotten teeth. I leave. The cleaning is done and we can go back inside. The nuts are watching TV. I cross the living room and finally enter my room. I slam the door shut. I'm indignant and I don't know why. The crazy guy who works at the pizza place is snoring in his bed like a saw cutting a piece of wood. I become more indignant. I go over to him and give him a kick in the behind. He awakens, frightened, and curls himself up in a corner.

"Listen, you son of a bitch!" I say to him. "Don't snore anymore!"

At the sight of his fear, my anger abates. I sit down on the bed again. I smell bad. So much so that I grab the towel and soap and head out toward the bathroom. On the way, I see old one-eyed Reyes, who is covertly urinating in a corner. I look around. I don't see anyone. I go over to Reyes and grab him tightly by the neck. I give him a kick in the testicles. I bang his head against the wall.

"Sorry, sorry . . . ," Reyes says.

I look at him, disgusted. His forehead is bleeding. Upon seeing this, I feel a strange pleasure. I grab the towel, twist it, and whip his frail chest.

"Have mercy . . . ," Reyes implores.

"Stop pissing everywhere!" I say furiously.

As I turn back down the hall, I see Arsenio there, leaning against the wall. He saw it all. He smiles. He leaves the can of beer in a corner and asks to borrow my towel. I give it to him. He twists it tightly. He makes a perfect whip of it and using all his strength brings it down on Reyes' back. One, two, three times, until the old man falls in a corner, bathed in urine, blood and sweat. Arsenio gives me the towel back. He smiles at me again. He grabs his can of beer and sits down again at his desk. Mr. Curbelo has left. Arsenio is now the head of the halfway house again.

I continue toward the bathroom. I go inside, lock the door and start to undress. My clothes stink, but my socks reek even more. I grab them, inhale their deeply embedded muddy smell, and throw them in the waste basket. They were the only socks I had. Now I'll walk around the city sockless.

I go in the shower, turn it on and stand under the hot water. As the water runs over my head and body, I smile, thinking of old Reyes. I'm amused by the face he made when he was beaten, by the way his frail body shuddered, by his sorrowful pleas. Then he fell on top of his own urine and asked for mercy from there. "Mercy!" Remembering that, my body shudders with pleasure again. I soap myself up thoroughly, using my underwear as a washcloth. Then I rinse myself off and turn off the shower. I dry off. I put on the same clothes. I go out. In the living room, the nuts are still watching TV. The set is broken and you can only see colored lights, but still they sit, watching the screen, paying the lack of images no mind. I go to my room and leave the towel and the soap. I go out, combing my hair, toward the living room. The nuts are still there, frozen in place as they watch the broken TV. I kneel before the set and fix it. I sit in the tattered armchair and prop my feet up on an empty chair. The announcer says something about ten guerrillas dead in El Salvador. Then Eddy, the nut who is well-versed in international politics, comes down to earth.

"That's it!" he yells. "Ten dead communists! There should be one hundred! One thousand! A million dead communists! Someone with some balls needs to wipe them out! First Mexico. Then Panama. Then Venezuela and Nicaragua. And then clean up the United States, which is infested with communists. They took everything from me! Everything!"

"Me, too." says Ida, the grande dame come to ruin. "Six houses, a pharmacy and an apartment building."

Then, Ida turns to Pino, the silent nut, and asks, "How about you, Pino, what did they take from you?"

But Pino doesn't answer. He looks out at the street and remains still, unblinking.

Just then, in comes old Castaño, the centenarian

who leans on the walls when he walks. Like one-eyed Reyes and that decrepit hag Hilda, urine permeates his clothes.

"I want to die!" Castaño yells. "I want to die!"

René, the youngest of the two mental retards, grabs him by the neck, shakes him forcefully, and takes him back to his room by kicking his behind.

"I want to die!" We hear old Castaño's voice again until René slams shut the door to his room, burying his screams. Then Napoleon, a four-foot-tall midget, fat and solid as a speed bag, comes over to me. Mother Nature placed a medieval knight's face on that midget's body. His face is tragically beautiful and his large, popping eyes forever wear a deeply submissive expression. He's Colombian, and his manner of speaking is also submissive—the speech of those born to obey.

"Sir, sir," he says to me. "That one!" and he points at a nut named Tato, whose face looks like a former boxer's. "That one touched me!"

"Stop talking shit." Tato says.

"He touched me," Napoleon insists. "Yesterday, in my room, he came at night and touched me!"

I look at Tato. He doesn't look like a homosexual. Nonetheless, the midget's words make him sweat in embarrassment. He sweats. He sweats. He sweats. He sweats so much that in three minutes his white shirt becomes transparent.

"Don't pay any attention to the nuts here," he says to me. "or you'll end up crazy, too."

"He touched me!" Napoleon keeps saying.

Then Tato gets up from his seat, laughs suddenly in an incomprehensible way and says to me carelessly, "That's the same thing they said to Rocky Marciano in the eighth round and he got up and knocked out Joe Wolcox. So . . . life sucks!" and he leaves.

Ida, the grande dame come to ruin, looks at me, outraged,

"The things we have to see!" she says. "The things we have to hear!"

The TV news hour is over. I get up. They call us to eat.

Caridad the *mulata* serves the food. She also served time, back in Cuba, for stabbing her husband. She lives across the street from the halfway house, with a new husband and two huge pedigree dogs. She feeds the dogs with food from the halfway house. Not leftovers, but hot food that she takes from the nuts' daily ration. The *locos* know it and don't complain. If they do complain, Caridad the *mulata* tells them as plain as day to go to hell. And nothing happens. Mr. Curbelo never finds out. Or if he does find out, he says, as always, "My employees have my complete confidence." So none of what you're saying is true. The nuts lose again and realize that it's best to keep their mouths shut. Caridad the *mulata* would like to make the stew every day so she can get Mr. Curbelo to pay her those good thirty dollars more. That's why she says to the nuts all the time, "Complain! Protest! Today's peas are inedible! The truth is that you're a bunch of pussies!"

But none of the nuts complain, and Curbelo saves his money by continuing to make the stew every day with his little bourgeois face.

"Do you want to move to a different table?" Caridad asks me at dinner time.

"Yes."

"Don't you like those disgusting *locos*?"

"No."

"Come on," she says, "sit here," and she swipes the midget Napoleon out of his seat and seats me in his place. And so I stop sitting at the untouchables' table, with Hilda, Reyes, Pepe and René. Now I'm at a table with Eddy, Tato, Pino, Pedro, Ida and Louie. That afternoon we had rice, raw lentils, three pieces of lettuce and *salpicón*. I had three spoonfuls and spit the fourth out onto my plate. I left. As I pass by Mr. Curbelo's desk, I see Arsenio eating. He's eating on a plastic tray, brought from a nearby diner. He's eating with a fork and knife, and his food is yellow rice, pork, *yuca* and red tomatoes. And beer, too.

"Hey," he says to me when I pass by. "Take a seat."

I sit down. He waves at me with his hand to wait until he's done. I wait. He finishes eating. He takes all the leftovers and throws them out, along with the tray, in the waste basket. The empty can of beer, too. He burps. He looks at me with lost eyes. He takes out a pack of cigarettes and offers me one. We smoke. Then he says, "Okay . . . let's get right to it. Do you want to be my assistant here?"

"No," I say. "I'm not interested."

"It will be great," he advises me.

"I'm not interested."

"Fine." he says. "Friends?"

"Friends." I say.

He shakes my hand.

"I am the way I am," he says. "I smoke marijuana, I drink beer, I do blow, I do it all! But I'm a man."

"I get you," I say.

"I see you give the old one-eyed man a beating and I could give a shit. Now, I expect the same of you. Everything you see me do around us stays between us men. Got it?"

"Got it," I say.

"Mafia?"

"Mafia," I reply.

"Great." He smiles.

I get up. I go to my room. I lie down on the bed. I don't like what just happened. I regret having beaten the old one-eyed man. But it's too late. I've gone from being a witness to being complicit in what happens in the halfway house.

I fell asleep. I dreamt that I was running na-ked along a wide avenue and that I was going into a house surrounded by a beautiful garden. It was Mr. Curbelo's house. I knocked at the door and his wife answered. She was a dish. She let me hug and kiss her. She said "I'll give you whatever you want. My name is Necessity."

"I'll call you Necess," I said. And I yelled loudly, "Necess!"

Then Curbelo pulled up in his gray car. I tried to escape through the garden, but he grabbed me by the arm. My body was covered in white scales.

"Here!" screamed Curbelo, and a police car showed up in the garden. That's when I woke up.

It was about twelve at night. The crazy guy who works in the pizza place snores like a pig. I head out, shirtless, toward the living room. There I find Arsenio and Ida, the grande dame come to ruin. Arsenio has his hand on her knee. He sticks his tongue in her ear. Ida resists. She sees me and resists even more. I pass by them and sit in the tattered armchair.

"Arsenio," Ida says angrily, "tomorrow I'm going to tell Mr. Curbelo everything."

Arsenio starts laughing. He touches one of her flaccid breasts. He presses himself against it.

"For God's sake!" Ida says. "Don't you realize I'm an old woman?"

"It's like cod," Arsenio says. "The older, the better."

Then he looks at me. He knows I'm looking at him and says to me, with all familiarity, "Mafia!"

"Mafia," I say. I light a cigarette and lean back in the armchair.

"Let me go, Arsenio," Ida begs. But Arsenio laughs. He tries to stick his hand under the old lady's dress. He kisses her on the mouth. "Please . . . ," says Ida.

"Let her go." I say. "Let her go already."

"Mafia?" Arsenio asks.

"Yeah, I'm part of your mafia, but leave the poor old lady alone already."

Arsenio laughs. He lets her go unexpectedly. Ida quickly leaves and shuts herself in her room. I hear her lock it from the inside.

"I am a beast, just like you," I then say, looking at the ceiling. "I'm a beast."

Arsenio gets up. He goes to his room. He throws himself onto the bed.

"Mafia!" he says from there. "Life is just one big mafia! No more."

I'm left all alone. I smoke my cigarette. Tato, the homosexual boxer, shows up. He sits in a chair in front of me. A ray of light bathes his pockmarked face.

"Listen to this," he says to me. "Listen to this story. Which is my story. The story of the avenger of a painful tragedy. The tragedy of a final melodrama without any prospects. The fatal coincidence of an endless tragedy. Listen to this, my story. The story of someone imperfect who thought he was perfect. And death's tragic end, which is life. What do you think?"

"Great," I say.

"That's enough!" he says, and leaves.

I fall asleep.

I dreamt about Fidel Castro. He was taking refuge in a white house. I was shooting at the house with a cannon. Fidel was in briefs and an undershirt. He was missing a few teeth. He was yelling insults at me out the windows. He was saying, "*Cabrón*! You'll never get me out of here!" I was frantic. The house was already in ruins but Fidel was still inside, moving around as agile as a mountain lion. "You won't get me out of here!" He yelled hoarsely. "You'll never get me out!" It was Fidel's last refuge. And even though I spent the whole dream shooting at him, I couldn't flush him out of those ruins. I wake up. It's already morning. I go to the bathroom. I urinate. Then I wash my face with cold water. I leave like that, dripping water, to go have breakfast. There's cold milk, cornflakes and sugar. I only drink milk. I go back to the TV and turn it on. I settle into the armchair again. The American preacher who talks about Jesus comes on the screen.

"You, sitting there in front of the TV," the preacher says. "Come now into the arms of the Lord."

My mouth becomes dry. I close my eyes. I try to imagine that yes, everything he says is true.

"Oh God!" I say, "Oh God, save me!"

I remain that way for ten or twelve seconds, with my eyes closed, waiting for the miracle of salvation. Then Hilda, the decrepit old hag, taps my shoulder.

"Do you have a cigarette?"

I give her one.

"You have very, very pretty eyes!" she says sweetly.

"Thank you."

"Don't mention it."

I get up. I don't know what to do. Go outside? Shut myself in my room? Sit on the porch? I go outside again. Go north? Go south? Who cares? I walk toward Flagler Street and then I turn to the left, going west, where the Cubans live. I walk on, I walk on, I walk on. I pass by dozens of bodegas, coffee shops, restaurants, barber shops, clothing stores, stores selling religious articles, tobacco shops, pharmacies, pawn shops. All of them are owned by Cuban petit bourgeois who arrived fifteen or twenty years ago, fleeing the communist regime. I stop in front of a shop mirror and comb my messy, straw-colored hair with my fingers. Then, it seems like someone is yelling "son of a bitch" at me. I turn around, furious. There's only an old blind man walking with a cane on the sidewalk. I walk on a little more along Flagler Street. I spend my last bit of change on a sip of coffee. I see a cigarette on the floor. I pick it up and bring it to my lips. Three women working in the coffee shop start laughing. I think they've seen me pick up the cigarette and I'm infuriated. It seems like one of them says, "There he goes! The wandering Jew!" I leave.

The sun beats down strongly on my head. Thick beads of sweat run like lizards down my chest and armpits. I walk on, I walk on, I walk on. Without looking anywhere in particular. Without searching for anything. Without going anywhere. I go into a church called San Juan Bosco. There's silence and air conditioning. I look around. Three believers are praying at the foot of the altar. An old woman stops before a statue of Jesus and touches his feet. Then she takes out a dollar and sticks it in an offering box. She lights a candle. She whispers her prayer. I walk along the aisle and sit in a pew at the back of the church. I take out the book of Romantic English poets and open it at random. It's a poem by John Clare, born in 1793, died in 1864 in the asylum of Northampton.

> I am: yet what I am none cares or knows,
> My friends forsake me like a memory lost;
> I am the self-consumer of my woes,
> They rise and vanish in oblivious host,
> Like shades in love and death's oblivion lost

I get up. I leave the church through the back. I walk along Flagler Street again. I pass by new barber shops, new restaurants, new clothing stores, pharmacies and drug stores. I walk on, I walk on, I walk on. My bones hurt, but I keep going. Until I stop at 23rd Avenue. I spread my arms. I look at the sun. It's time to go back to the halfway house.

*　　　*　　　*

I wake up. I've been here a month in the halfway house. My sheet is the same, my pillowcase, too. The towel that Mr. Curbelo gave me the first day is now filthy and damp and smells strongly of sweat. I take it and throw it around my neck. I go to the bathroom to wash up and urinate. I urinate on a checked shirt that some nut stuck in the toilet. Then I go over to the sink and turn one of the faucets. I splash cold water on my face. I dry off with the filthy towel. I go back to my room and sit on the bed. The nut who sleeps next to me is still sleeping. He sleeps in the nude and his giant member has an erection. The door opens and Josefina, the cleaning lady, comes in. She starts laughing, looking at the nut's member. "It looks like a spear," she says. And she calls out to Caridad, who is in the kitchen. Caridad pops in the door and takes my grimy towel and makes a whip out of it. She lifts it and brings it down forcefully on the nut's member. He jumps on the bed and yells, "They want to kill me!"

The two women start to laugh.

"Put that thing away, you shameless fool," Caridad says, "or I'm going to cut it off!"

The two women leave, discussing the nut's member.

"It's a spear," Josefina says with admiration.

I walk out after them toward the dining room, where Arsenio is handing out breakfast. I drink a glass of cold milk quickly and go back to the TV room to watch my favorite preacher.

There's a new crazy woman sitting in front of the set. She must be my age. Her body, while cheated by life, still has some curves. I sit next to her. I look around. There's no one. Everyone is at breakfast. I reach my hand out to the *loca* and put it on her knee.

"Yes, my angel," she says, without looking at me.

I raise my hand and get as far as her thighs. She lets me touch her without a complaint. I think the television preacher is talking about Corinthians now, about Paul, about the Thessalonians.

I raise my hand a little more and reach the crazy woman's sex. I squeeze it.

"Yes, my angel," she says without taking her eyes off the television.

"What's your name?" I ask.

"Frances, my angel."

"When did you get here?"

"Yesterday."

I start stroking her sex with my nails.

"Yes, my angel," she says. "Whatever you want, my angel."

I realize that she's trembling fearfully. I stop touching her. I feel pity for her. I take one of her hands and kiss it.

"Thank you, my angel," she says absentmindedly.

Arsenio comes in. He's done handing out breakfast and he comes to the TV with his usual can of beer. He drinks. He looks at the new crazy woman, amused.

"Mafia," he then says to me. "What do you think of our new acquisition?"

He puts a bare foot on Frances' knee. Then he puts the tip of his foot between the woman's thighs, trying to drill into her sex.

"Yes, my angel," says Frances, without taking her eyes off the television. "Whatever you want, my angels."

She trembles. She's trembling so much that it looks like the bones in her shoulders are going to come off. At that moment, the preacher is talking about a woman who had a vision of paradise.

"There were horses there . . . ," he says. "Tame horses grazing on grass that was always delicate, always green . . ."

"Mafia!" Arsenio screams at the television preacher. "Even you are in the mafia!"

He takes another sip of beer and leaves.

Frances closes her eyes, still trembling. She leans her head on the back of the sofa. I look around and there's no one. I get up from my chair and get on top of her gently. I put my hands around her neck and start squeezing.

"Yes, my angel," she says with her eyes closed.

I squeeze harder.

"Keep going, my angel."

I squeeze harder. Her face becomes a deep shade of red. Her eyes tear up. But she remains that way, meek, uncomplaining.

"My angel . . . my angel . . . ," she says in a small voice.

Then I stop squeezing. I take a deep breath. I look at her. I feel pity for her again. I take one of her emaciated hands and kiss it all over. Upon seeing her like that, so defenseless, I feel like hugging her and crying. She remains still, leaning her head on the back of her seat. With her eyes closed. Her mouth trembles. Her cheeks, too. I leave.

Mr. Curbelo has arrived and he talks to a friend on the phone.

When he talks on the phone, Mr. Curbelo sits back in his chair and puts his feet on his desk. He looks like a sultan.

"The competition was yesterday," Mr. Curbelo tells his friend through the phone receiver. "I came in second place. This time I shot with a sling speargun. I got a fifty-pound jewfish!"

Just then, old one-eyed Reyes goes up to Curbelo and asks for a cigarette.

"Shoo, shoo!" Mr. Curbelo waves him away with his hand. "Can't you see that I'm working?"

Reyes recoils toward the hallway. He hides behind a door. He looks all around with his one eye and, sure that no one can see him, takes his penis out and starts to urinate on the floor. That's Reyes' revenge. Urinating. And a storm of the most brutal beatings can come down on him, but he will always urinate in his room, in the living room and on the porch. People complain to Mr. Curbelo, but he won't kick him out of the boarding home. Reyes, according to him, is a good customer. He doesn't eat; he doesn't ask for his thirty-eight dollars; he doesn't demand clean towels or sheets. All he does is drink water, ask for cigarettes and urinate. I go to my room and throw myself on the bed. I think of Frances, the new little crazy woman whom I nearly suffocated a few minutes ago. I become angry with myself as I recall her defenseless face, her trembling body, her sad voice that never asked for forgiveness.

"Keep going, my angel, keep going . . ."

My feelings about her are a confusing mix of pity, hate, tenderness and cruelty.

Arsenio comes in the room and takes a seat in a chair next to my bed. He takes a can of beer out of his pocket and starts to drink.

"Mafia . . . ," he says to me, looking over my head toward the street. "What's life all about, mafia?"

I don't answer. I sit up in bed and also look out the window. A homosexual dressed as a woman walks by. Then a black sports car goes by, with its radio at full blast. Scandalous rock music invades the street for a few seconds. Then it starts fading as the car gets farther away. Arsenio goes over to the dresser belonging to the crazy guy who works at the pizza place and starts to root through his things. He takes out a shirt and some dirty pants and throws them on the floor. He comes upon a drawer with a lock on it, but he takes a screwdriver out of his pocket and inserts it between the lock and the wood. He pulls hard. The screws give. Arsenio opens the drawer and searches anxiously among the nut's papers, soaps and combs. Finally, he pulls a leather wallet out. He opens it and grabs a twenty-dollar bill. It's the nut's earnings from six days of work. He shows it to me. He smiles. He kisses it.

"Tonight we're going to eat well," he says. "Pizza, beer, cigarettes and coffee."

I look at him, speechless.

"Mafia!" he yells at me with a smile. He takes a swig of beer and leaves the room.

I'm left alone. I don't know what to do. I start looking out the window. A group of ten or twelve members of a religious order dressed immaculately in white go by. The homosexual dressed as a woman goes by again, this time on the arm of an enormous black man. And cars, cars, cars go by with their radios at full blast. I leave my room without any particular destination. Mr. Curbelo is still talking to his friend about yesterday's competition.

"They gave me a plaque," he says. "I hung it with the rest of them on the living room wall."

The house smells of urine. I go and sit in front of the television set, next to Frances again. I take her hand. I kiss it. She looks at me with her trembling smile.

"You look like him," she says.

"Who?"

"My little son's father."

I get up. I kiss her on the forehead. I hug her head tightly in my arms for a few minutes. Then, when my tenderness is exhausted, I look at her with irritation. Once again, I feel like harming her. I look around. There's no one. I put my hands on her neck and start to squeeze slowly.

"Yes, my angel, yes," she says, with a trembling smile.

I squeeze more. I squeeze hard, with all of my strength.

"Keep going, keep going . . . ," she says, in a small voice.

Then I let go. She has passed out and falls sideways in her seat. I take her face between my hands and start kissing her forehead madly. Little by little, she comes to. She looks at me. She smiles weakly. That's enough for me.

I leave. I pass by Curbelo's desk. He's done talking on the phone already.

"William!" he calls out to me. I go over to him. He takes a bottle of pills out of a drawer and grabs two.

"Open your mouth," he says.

I open it. He throws two pills inside: clack-clack.

"Swallow," he says.

I swallow.

"Can I leave now?"

"Yes. Find Reyes for me and bring him over so he can have his pills too."

I go to Reyes' room. He's lying down on a sheet soaked in urine. His room smells like a latrine.

"Listen, pig," I say, punching him in the sternum. "Curbelo wants to see you."

"Me? Me?"

"Yes, you, you filthy pig."

"Okay."

I leave holding my nose. I go to my room and throw myself on the bed. I look at the blue, peeling ceiling covered with small cockroaches. This is the end of me. I, William Figueras, who read all of Proust when I was fifteen years old, Joyce, Miller, Sartre, Hemingway, F. Scott Fitzgerald, Albee, Ionesco, Beckett. I who lived twenty years within the revolution, as its victimizer, witness, victim. Great.

Just then, someone pops up in my bedroom window. It's *El Negro*.

"Are you sleeping?"

"No, I'll be right out."

I button my shirt, smooth my hair with my fingers and go out to the garden.

"Hey," *El Negro* says when he sees me. "If you were sleeping, keep sleeping!"

"No," I say. "It's okay."

We sit down on some steps, at the foot of a closed door. There we shake hands effusively.

"How's that life of yours in Miami?" I ask.

"Same old, same old," *El Negro* says. "Oh!" he suddenly remembers. "Carlos Alfonso, the poet, went to Cuba. He was there for two weeks."

"And what does he have to say? What does he have to say about Cuba?"

"He says everything's the same. People are wearing jeans on the streets. Everyone in jeans!"

I burst out laughing.

"What else?"

"What else? Nothing," El Negro says. "Everything's the same. Everything is just as we left it five years ago. Except, perhaps, Havana is in ruins. But everything's the same."

Then *El Negro* looks me right in the eye and slaps my knee with his hand.

"Willy," he says to me, "let's leave here!"

"Where to?"

"To Madrid. To Spain. Let's go see the Gothic neighborhood in Barcelona. Let's go see El Greco in the Cathedral of Toledo!"

I start laughing.

"Someday we'll go, yeah . . . ," I say, laughing.

"With only five thousand dollars," says *El Negro*. "Five thousand dollars! We'll retrace *allll* of Hemingway's steps in *The Sun Also Rises*."

"Someday we'll go," I say.

We're silent for a few seconds. A nut comes over and asks us for a cigarette. *El Negro* gives it to him.

"I want to see where Brett... you remember Brett Ashley, don't you? The heroine from *A Moveable Feast*."

"Yes," I say. "I remember."

"I want to see where Brett ate; where Brett danced; where Brett screwed the bullfighter," *El Negro* says, smiling at the horizon.

"You'll see it," I say, "Someday you'll see it!"

"Let's make our goal two years," *El Negro* says. "In two years, we'll go to Madrid."

"Okay," I say. "Two years. Okay."

El Negro looks me right in the eye again. He slaps me on the knee affectionately. I realize he's about to leave. He gets up, takes a nearly full pack of Marlboros out of his pocket and gives it to me. Then he takes out two quarters and gives them to me, too.

"Write something, Willy," he says.

"I'll try," I say.

He bursts out laughing. He turns on his heels. He gets farther away. When he gets to the corner, he turns around and yells something to me. It seems like part of a poem, but I only hear the words "dust," "silhouettes," "symmetry." That's all.

I go back inside the halfway house.

In my room, I throw myself back on the bed and fall asleep again. This time I dreamt that the Revolution was over, and that I was returning to Cuba with a group of old octogenarians. An old man with a long, white beard guided us, outfitted with a long staff. We stopped every three steps and the old man pointed out a bunch of ruins with his staff.

"This was the Sans Souci Cabaret," the old man then said.

We walked on a little bit and then he would say again, "This was the Capitol building," pointing at a field of weeds full of broken chairs.

"This was the Hilton Hotel," and the old man pointed at a bunch of red bricks.

"This was the Paseo del Prado," and now it was just a lion statue half-sunk into the ground.

So we walked through all of Havana like that. Vegetation covered everything, like in the bewitched city in Sleeping Beauty. Over everything reigned an air of silence and mystery akin to what Columbus must have found when he first landed on Cuban soil.

I woke up.

It had to be about one in the morning. I sit on the edge of the bed with an empty feeling in my chest. I look out the window. There are three homosexuals dressed as women on the corner, waiting for lonely men. Cars driven by these men without women prowl around the corner slowly. I rise from the bed, depressed. I don't know what to do. The crazy guy who works at the pizza place is sleeping under a thick blanket, even though the heat is unbearable. He's snoring. I decide to go out to the living room and sit in the old, tattered armchair. I go. As I pass by Arsenio's room, I hear the voice of Hilda, the decrepit old hag, who is complaining because Arsenio is messing around with her behind.

"Keep still!" Arsenio says. I hear them struggle. I reach the armchair and sink heavily into it. Louie, the American, is sitting in a dark corner of the room.

"Leave me alone!" he says to the wall, his voice full of hate. "I'm going to destroy you! Leave me alone!"

I hear Hilda's frantic voice coming from Arsenio's room again.

"Not there," she says. "Not there!"

Tato, the ex-boxer, comes out of the shadows wearing only a small pair of briefs. He sits in a chair in front of me and asks for a cigarette. I give it to him. He lights it with a cheap lighter.

"Listen to this story, Willy," he says to me as he exhales a cloud of smoke. "Listen to this story, you're gonna like it. Back there, in Havana, in the age of Jack Dempsey, there was a man who wanted to be the avenger of mankind. They called him 'The God of the Starry Skies,' 'The King of the Underworld,' 'The Terrible Man.'"

He's quiet for a few seconds, then he reveals:

"That man was me."

He lets out an incoherent peal of laughter and repeats,

"Do you like my story, Willy?"

"Yes."

"It's the story of complete revenge. Of all mankind. Of a man's pain. Do you get it?"

"Yes."

"Great," he says, getting up. "Tomorrow I'll tell you the next chapter."

He takes a long drag of his cigarette and disappears in the dark again.

It's hot. I take off my shirt and put my feet on a beaten-up chair. I close my eyes, sink my chin into my chest and remain that way for many seconds, immersed in the wide emptiness of my existence.

I point an imaginary gun at my temple. I shoot.

"Fuck you up your ass!" Louie yells at his ghosts. "Fuck your ass!"

I get up. I return slowly to my room. In the half-light I see two cockroaches, as big as dates, fornicating on my pillow. I grab my towel, twist it and bring it down heavily on them. They escape. I fall on the bed, splaying my legs. I touch myself. It has been one long year since I've been inside a woman. The last one was a Colombian *loca* I met in a hospital. I think of the Colombian. I remember the surprising way she took her bra off in front of me, in her room, and showed me her tits. Then I remember the shameless way she pulled down the sheet covering her, and showed me her sex, and how she then opened her legs slowly and said to me, "Come here."

I was afraid since the hospital nurses went in and out of the rooms constantly. But the pull of sex was stronger. I fell on her. I entered her slowly, sweetly. She had a beautiful whore's mouth.

I wake up. It's daytime already. The heat is suffocating, but the crazy guy who works at the pizza place sleeps under a thick blanket that reeks like a dead animal. I look at him with hate. I entertain myself imagining for a few seconds wielding a sharp axe over his square head. When the hate starts gnawing at me, I stand up, look for my filthy towel and a sliver of soap and go to the bathroom. The bathroom is flooded. Somebody put a leather jacket in the toilet. The floor is covered in feces, paper and other filth. I head for the second bathroom in the other hallway of the halfway house. Everyone is waiting in front of it: René, Pepe, Hilda, Ida, Pedro and Eddy. Louie, the American, has been inside the bathroom for an hour and doesn't want to come out. Eddy beats on the door loudly. But Louie won't open.

"Fuck you! Go fuck yourself!" He yells from inside.

Then Pepe, the older of the two mental retards, lets out a terrifying scream, lowers his pants, and defecates right there, in the hallway, in plain view of everyone.

Eddy, the nut who is well-versed in international politics, kicks on the bathroom door again.

"Leave me alone, you fucking chicken!" Louie screams from inside.

I leave. I go to the garden and urinate behind an areca palm. Then I wash my hands and my face in a gush of water coming out of a spigot. I go back in the halfway house and hear the ruckus in front of the bathroom still going on. I go over there and arrive just as Eddy, the nut who is well-versed in politics, throws his entire body against the bathroom door and busts the lock. Louie, the American, is sitting on the toilet, wiping his behind with a raincoat.

"It's him!" Eddy yells. "He's the one who sticks clothes and cardboard in the toilets!"

Louie howls like a trapped animal. He puts on his pants quickly and hurls himself at Eddy, punching him in the mouth. Eddy falls to the floor with bloody lips. Louie shoves his way through the *locos* and leaves the crowd for the living room. He howls like a mad wolf.

"Go eat your chicken feed, chickens!" he shouts from the living room. He opens the front door forcefully, yells more curses and goes outside slamming the door so hard that three or four glass panes fall to the floor in pieces.

"Son of a bitch!" Eddy screams, his mouth bloody. "Now they'll finally kick you out!"

Ida, the grande dame come to ruin, comes over to me with an angry expression and takes on a confidential tone of voice:

"Curbelo won't kick him out. Don't you see that Louie receives a check for six-hundred dollars every month? He's the best customer here. He could be a crazy murderer and he'd never get kicked out."

Arsenio goes over to the bathroom. The nuts' screams have woken him up. His eyes are glassy, and his long, wiry hair is standing straight up and looks like a huge metal helmet. He looks at the blood on the floor, at Pepe's huge pile of shit, at Eddy's broken mouth, at the rain coat stuffed in the toilet, all with indifference. It's nothing new. It's all part of everyday life at the halfway house. He scratches his robust chest. He spits on the floor. He burps. He shrugs his shoulders and declares,

"You really are animals!"

He turns around and walks slowly to the living room.

"Breakfast!" he screams from there at the top of his lungs and the nuts fall over each other to follow him to the dining room. I don't feel like drinking cold milk. I need coffee. I search my pockets. All I have is a dime. I go to my room and stop in front of the bed belonging to the crazy guy who works at the pizza place. I take his shirt from the top of the wardrobe and search the pockets. Then I grab his pants and do the same. I find a quarter and half a pack of cigarettes. I put it all in my pocket and go out to the corner coffee shop. On the way, I run into Louie, the American, who is avidly going through a garbage can. A little further on, Hilda, the decrepit old hag, lifts up her dress right in the middle of the street and urinates next to a bus stop. On the bus stop's bench, a young vagrant is sleeping with his head propped up on a dirty backpack. Two huge dogs cross the road toward Flagler Street. Cars race by toward downtown. I get to the coffee shop and ask for coffee. They give it to me cold since they know I live in the halfway house and I won't complain. I could protest, but I don't. I drink the coffee in one gulp. I pay and return to the boarding home. It's time to listen to my preacher, so I turn on the TV and slump into the tattered armchair. The preacher comes on the screen. He's talking about a rock 'n' roll star who threw his guitar down in the middle of a concert and proclaimed, "Save me, Lord!"

"He's a well-known star," the preacher says. "I don't have to name names. But that guy . . . still young, sick of acting, up to here with living a lie, threw his guitar to the ground and proclaimed 'Save me!' And I said, 'Satan, squalor of darkness . . . you can't fool a man who has called for Him. Hallelujah!'"

The preacher is crying. His audience is also crying.

"There's still time," the preacher says. "There's still time to come to the Lord."

Just then, a strong whiff of cologne water reaches me. I turn around and see Frances, the new little *loca*, sitting in a chair behind me. She has made up her face carefully and is wearing a thin blue dress that makes her look younger. Her hair is all done up. And her skin looks clean and fresh. I look at her legs. They're still pretty. I get up from my seat and go over to her. I take her hands and examine them carefully. They're clean and elegant, although her nails are too long and unkempt. Then, I open her mouth with my fingers. She's just missing a few molars. I look around and don't see anyone. I kneel on the floor and lift her skirt. I sink my head in between her legs. She smells good. I sit her back in the chair again. I take off her shoes and examine her feet. They're small and pink and also smell clean. Then I stand. I hug her. I kiss her neck, her ears, her mouth.

"Frances!" I say. "Oh, Frances!"

"Yes, my angel," she says.

"Oh, Frances!"

"Yes, my angel, yes . . ."

I take her by the hand and take her to her room. It's the women's room and it has a lock on the inside. We go in. I lock the door. I take her gently over to the bed and remove her shoes.

"Oh, Frances!" I say, kissing her feet.

"Yes, my angel."

Hastily, I remove her panties. I spread her legs. She has pretty brown fuzz. I kiss it anxiously. While I kiss her, I take out my throbbing sex. I know that the minute I enter her, I'll ejaculate. But I don't care.

"Frances," I say. "Frances."

I start to penetrate her slowly. While I do so, I kiss her frantically on the mouth. Then I shudder to the very marrow of my bones and a wave of lava comes from deep inside of me and floods her inside.

"Yes, my angel." Frances says.

And I lie there, as if I were dead, with my ear to her chest. I feel her delicate hand beating softly on my back, as if I were a newborn who had hiccupped at the breast.

"Yes, my angel, yes . . ."

I pull out. I sit on the edge of the bed. I take my hand to her very thin neck and squeeze slowly.

"Yes, my angel, yes . . ."

I close my eyes. I take a deep breath. I squeeze a little more.

"Yes . . . yes . . ."

I squeeze tighter. Until she gets red in the face and her eyes fill up with tears. Then I stop squeezing.

"Oh, Frances!" I say, kissing her sweetly on the mouth.

I get up from the bed and straighten my pants. She straightens her clothes and also jumps up from the bed, searching for her shoes with her feet. I leave the room and go back to the tattered armchair to watch my favorite preacher again. It's the end of the show. The preacher, seated at a piano, sings the blues with a splendid black man's voice:

> There's just one way
> And it's not easy to get there
> Oh Lord!
> I know.
> I know.
> I know it's not easy to reach You.

Mr. Curbelo arrived at ten. He goes directly to the kitchen where Caridad, Josefina and another employee named Tía, who occasionally cleans up the retards Pepe and René, are waiting for him. They meet. From the porch, I see Curbelo talking to his employees with gusto. Then he claps his hands and they disperse. All of a sudden, everything's a rush of frantic activity. Arsenio runs around the rooms placing large rolls of toilet paper at the foot of every bed. Caridad the *mulata* sends Pino, the peon, to bring, as a matter of urgency, a piece of ham for the stew from the bodega. Josefina runs from room to room armed with a broom to clear the cobwebs from the corners and ceilings. Tía, loaded down with sheets and clean towels, runs quickly through the halls changing dirty, pissed-on bed sheets. Curbelo himself breezes easily through the living room and lays new rugs, brought hastily from his own house, down over the dirty, peeling floor.

"Inspection!" Tía says as she walks by me. "Today government inspectors are coming!"

And so tablecloths are laid over the tables, a water fountain is installed, clean clothes are given out to the more terrifying cases, such as Reyes, Castaño and Hilda. Perfume is sprayed on the old, sweat-stained furniture and new silverware, wrapped in fine cloth napkins, is placed on the dining room table in front of every chair.

"The old fox!" says Ida, the grande dame come to ruin, who stands next to me and eyes Curbelo with hatred as he straightens up, cleans and disguises everything. "He's the most repulsive thing here."

I believe it. I also watch that old sleazebag, hating his bourgeois face and voice, and how he sponges up what little blood is left in our veins. I also think that you have to be made of the same stuff as hyenas or vultures to own this halfway house.

I stand up. I don't know what to do. I go toward my room slowly in search of the book of English poets. I want to reread poems by John Clare, the crazy poet from Northampton. As I turn down the hall that leads to my room, I see old one-eyed Reyes urinating in a corner like a frightened dog. As I walk by him, I raise my hand and bring it down forcefully on his frail shoulder. He shudders, terrified.

"Mercy . . . ," he says. "Have mercy on me."

I look at him, disgusted. His glass eye swims in yellow pus. His whole body reeks of urine.

"How old are you?" I ask.

"Sixty-five," he says.

"What did you used to do in Cuba?"

"I sold clothes, in a store."

"Did you live well?"

"Yes."

"How so?"

"I had my own house, a wife, a car . . ."

"What else?"

"On Sundays, I played tennis at the Havana Yacht Club. I used to dance. I went to parties."

"Do you believe in God?"

"Yes, I believe in our Lord Jesus Christ."

"Will you go to heaven?"

"I think so."

"Will you also urinate up there?"

He is silent. Then he looks at me with a pained smile.

"I won't be able to avoid it," he says.

I bring my fist up again and let it fall on his dirty, unkempt head forcefully. I'd like to kill him.

"Have mercy, man," he says to me, exaggerating his anguish. "Have mercy on me."

"What was your favorite song when you were young?"

"*Blue Moon*," he replies without hesitation.

I don't say anything more. I turn my back on him and continue on to my room. I get to my bed and look for the book of English Romantic poets under my pillow. I stick it in my pocket and head back out to the porch. As I pass the women's room, I see Frances sitting on her bed, drawing something on a piece of paper. I get closer. She stops drawing and looks at me, smiling sadly.

"Worthless things," she says, showing me her work.

I take it in my hands. It's a portrait of Mr. Curbelo. It's done in the style of primitive artists. It's very good, and it admirably reflects the stinginess and smallness of the subject. She hasn't left out the desk, the telephone and the pack of Pall Malls that Curbelo always has out in front of him. Everything is exact. It also breathes its own life, that childish, captivating life that only a primitive's drawings can transmit.

"I have more," she says, opening a folder. I take them all and leaf though them.

"They're quite good!" I say.

There they (we) all are, the halfway house's inhabitants. Caridad, the *mulata* whose hardened face still retains a distant flicker of goodness. There's one-eyed Reyes, with his glass eye and his fox's smile. There's Eddy, the nut who is well-versed in international politics, with his ever-present expression of impotence and bottled rage. There's Tato, with his groggy boxer's face and his lost look. And there's Arsenio, with his devilish eyes. And there I am, with a face that is both hardened and sad at the same time. She's really good! She has captured all of our souls.

"Do you know that you're a good painter?"

"No," says Frances. "I have no technique."

"No," I say to her. "You're already a painter. Your technique is primitive, but it's very good."

She takes her drawings out of my hands and puts them back in the folder.

"They're worthless," she says with a sad smile.

"Listen," I say, sitting down next to her. "I swear that . . . pay attention. Let me say this to you and believe me, please. You are a tremendous artist. You are. I'm telling you. I'm here, in this disgusting *house*, and I'm practically a phantom of myself. But I'm telling you that I know something about art. You are amazing. Do you know who Rousseau was?"

"No," she says.

"Well you don't need to," I say. "Your technique is similar. Have you ever painted oils?"

"No."

"Learn to paint with oils," I say. "Give some color to these drawings. Listen!" I say, taking her strongly by the neck. "You are a good artist. Goooood."

She smiles. I squeeze my hand a little tighter and her eyes fill with tears. But she keeps smiling. I feel a wave of desire washing over me again. I let go of her. I go over to the room's door and lock it again. I go over to her gently and start to kiss her arms, her armpits, the nape of her neck. She smiles. I kiss her slowly on the mouth. Once again, I throw her down on the bed and take out my penis. Pulling aside her small panties with my fingers, I penetrate her slowly.

"Kill me," she says.

"You really want me to kill you?" I ask, sinking into her completely.

"Yes, kill me," she says.

I get a hand on her neck and start to squeeze forcefully again.

"Bitch!" I say, suffocating her and penetrating her at the same time. "You're a good artist. You draw well. But you need to learn about color. Colooor."

"*Ay!*" she says.

"Die!" I say, feeling myself dissolve between her legs again.

We remain that way for a while, totally undone.

I'm kissing her cold hand. She's playing with my hair. I stand up. I straighten my shirt. She lowers her dress and sits on the edge of the bed.

"Listen," I say to her. "Do you want to go for a spin with me?"

"Where to, my angel?"

"Around!"

"Okay."

We leave. When we get to the street, Frances presses against me and grabs my arm.

"Where are we going?" she says.

"I don't know."

I look up and down the street. Then I point vaguely at a place they call Little Havana. We start to walk. This might be the poorest ghetto of the Cuban section. Here live the great majority of the 50,000 who arrived on Miami's shores in that last spectacular exodus of 1980. They haven't been able to get a leg up yet, and you can see them any time of day sitting in the doorways of their homes, sporting shorts, brightly colored t-shirts and baseball hats. They flaunt thick gold chains on their necks with medallions of saints, Indians and stars. They drink canned beer. They fix their rundown cars and listen, for hours on end, to loud rock or exasperating drum solos on their portable radios.

We walk. When we get to 8th Street, we turn to

the right and head toward the heart of the ghetto. Bodegas, clothing stores, opticians, barber shops, restaurants, coffee shops, pawn shops, furniture stores. All of it small, square, simple, made without any architectural artifice or aesthetic concerns. Created to make a few cents and thus cobble together that petit bourgeois lifestyle to which the average Cuban aspires.

We walk on. We walk on. When we reach the big, gray arcade of a Baptist church, we sit at the foot of one of the pillars. A protest march of old people passes on the street, toward downtown. I don't know what they're marching for. They raise signs that say, "Enough already!" and they're waving Cuban and American flags. Somebody comes over to us and gives us both typewritten pieces of paper. I read:

> It's time. The "Cuban Avengers" group has been started in Miami. From today on, take heed all the indifferent, the mean-spirited, the closet communists and all those who enjoy life in this hedonistic and bucolic city while an unhappy Cuba moans in chains. "Cuban Avengers" will show all Cubans the path to follow.

I crumple up the piece of paper and throw it out. I start laughing. I lean against the pillar and look at Frances. She gets closer to me and sinks her shoulder into my ribs. She takes one of my arms and places it over her shoulder. I squeeze her a little more and kiss her head.

"My angel," she says. "Were you ever a communist?"

"Yes."

"Me too."

We're silent. Then she says,

"At the beginning."

I lean my head back against the pillar and sing an old anthem from the early years of the Revolution in a low voice:

> *Somos las brigadas Conrado Benítez*
> *Somos la vanguardia de la revolución*[1]

She continues:

> *Con el libro en alto, cumplimos una meta*
> *Llevar a toda Cuba la alfabetización*[2]

We burst out laughing.

"I taught five peasants how to read," she confesses.

"Oh yeah? Where?"

"In the Sierra Maestra," she says. "In a place called El Roble."

"I was around there," I say. "I was teaching some other peasants in La Plata. Three mountains from there."

---

[1] We're the Conrado Benítez brigade, we're the vanguard of the Revolution

[2] With our books raised, we meet the goal of bringing literacy to everyone in Cuba

"How long ago was that, my angel?"

I close my eyes.

"Twenty-two . . . twenty-three years ago," I say.

"Nobody understands that," she says. "I tell my psychiatrist and he just gives me strong Etrafon pills. Twenty-three years, my angel?"

She looks at me with tired eyes.

"I think I'm dead inside," she says.

"Me too."

I take her by the hands and we stand up. A black convertible goes by in front of us. A Miami teenager sticks his head out and yells at us, "Trash!"

I flash him the longest finger on my hand. Then I squeeze Frances' hand and we start walking back to the halfway house. I'm hungry. I'd like to eat, at the very least, a meat empanada. But I don't have a single cent.

"I have two dimes," says Frances, untying a handkerchief.

"They're no good. Everything in this country costs more than twenty-five cents."

Nonetheless, we stop in front of a coffee shop called *La Libertaria*.

"How much is that empanada?" Frances asks an old server who looks bored behind the counter.

"Fifty cents."

"Oh!"

We turn around. When we've gone a few steps, the man calls out to us.

"Are you hungry?"

"Yes," I reply.

"Are you Cuban?"

"Yes."

"Man and wife?"

"Yes."

"Come in, I'll give you something to eat."

We go in.

"My name is Montoya," the man says as he cuts two big slices of bread and starts to put ham and cheese on them. "I've also had rough times in this country. Don't tell anyone I said so, but this country will *eat you alive*. I'm Montoya!" He says again, adding two large pickle slices between the bread slices. "I'm an old revolutionary. I've been imprisoned under every one of the tyrannies Cuba has suffered. In 1933, in 1952 and most recently, under the hammer and sickle."

"Anarchist?" I ask.

"Anarchist," he confesses. "My whole life. Fighting the Americans and the Russians. Now I'm very peaceful."

He puts the open-faced sandwiches, all ready, on the counter and invites us to eat. Then he takes out two Coca-Colas and sets them in front of us.

"In 1961," he says, leaning forward on his elbows over the counter, "Rafael Porto Penas, lame Estrada, the now-deceased Manolito Ruvalcaba, and I were all together in the same car with Fidel Castro. I was at the wheel. Fidel was without his bodyguards. Lame Estrada looked him right in the eye and asked, 'Fidel . . . are you a communist?' And Fidel replied, '*Caballeros*, I swear to you by my mother that I am not a communist nor will I ever be one!' See what kind of guy he is!"

We burst out laughing.

"Cuban history isn't written yet," Montoya says. "The day I write it, the world will end!"

He goes over to two customers who just walked in and Frances and I take the opportunity to eat our sandwiches. We eat and drink in silence for a few minutes. When we're done, Montoya is in front of us again.

"Thank you," I say.

He stretches his hand out to me. Then he extends it to Frances.

"Go to Homestead!" he then says. "They need people there to pick avocadoes and tomatoes."

"Thank you," I say again. "Maybe we'll do that."

We leave. We walk toward First Street. While we walk, a great idea pops into my head.

"Frances," I say, stopping at Sixth Avenue.

"Tell me, my angel."

"Frances . . . Frances . . . ," I say, leaning up against a wall and bringing her gently to me. "I've just had a magnificent idea."

"What's that?"

"Let's leave the halfway house!" I say, bringing her to my chest. "With what we both receive from social security, we could live in a small house, and we could even earn a little more if we did some menial work here and there."

She looks at me, surprised by my idea. Her mouth and chin start trembling slightly.

"My angel!" she says, moved. "And can I bring my little boy from New Jersey?"

"Of course!"

"And you would help me raise him?"

"Yes!"

She squeezes my hands tightly. She looks at me with her trembling smile. She's so moved that for a few seconds, she doesn't know what to say. Then all the color drains from her face. Her eyes roll back and she faints in my arms.

"Frances ... Frances!" I say, helping her up from the sidewalk. "What's wrong?"

I pat her face a few times. Slowly, she comes to.

"It's hope, my angel ... ," she says. "Hope!"

She hugs me tightly. I look at her. Her lips, her cheeks, her face, all of it is trembling intensely. She starts to cry.

"It's not going to work out," she says. "It's not going to work out."

"Why?"

"Because I'm crazy. I need to take four pills of strong Etrafon daily."

"I'll give them to you."

"I hear voices," she says. "It seems like everyone is talking about me."

"Me too," I say. "But to hell with the voices!"

I grab her by the waist. Slowly, we begin to walk

back to the halfway house. A new car passes next to us. A guy with a thin beard and tinted glasses sticks his head out the window and yells at me, "Dump that bitch!"

We walk on. While we walk, I'm planning the steps we'll take. Tomorrow, the first of the month, our social security checks arrive. I'll talk to Curbelo and ask him for mine and Frances'. Then we'll pack our bags, I'll call a taxi and we'll go house hunting. For the first time in years, a small ray of hope shines into the deep dark well of my empty chest. Without realizing it, I smile.

We enter the halfway house through the back porch, cocooned by dark metallic fabric. The nuts have finished eating and are digesting there, sitting on the wooden chairs. Upon entering the house, Frances and I separate. She goes to her room; I go on to mine. I'm singing an old Beatles song:

> *He's a real nowhere man*
> *Sitting in his nowhere land*

Hilda, the decrepit old hag, steps in front of me and asks for a cigarette. I give it to her. Then I grab her head and give her a kiss on the cheek.

"Thank you!" she says, surprised. "That's the first kiss I've gotten in mannnnny years."

"Do you want another one?"

"Okay."

I kiss her again, on the other cheek.

"Why, thank you," she says to me.

I continue on my way, singing *Nowhere Man*. I get to my room. The crazy guy who works at the pizza place is on his bed, counting his money.

"Hey," I say to him: "I need you to give me a dollar."

"A dollar, Mister William? You're crazy!"

I pry his wallet from his hands. I look for a dollar. I take it.

"Give me my wallet," the crazy guy groans.

I give it to him, then throw my arm around him affectionately.

"A dollar, man. Just a lousy dollar." I say to him.

He looks at me. I smile at him. I kiss his face. He ends up laughing himself.

"Okay, Mister William," he says.

"I'll pay you back tomorrow," I say.

I go outside, toward the corner. I'm going to buy today's paper to look through the ads for a good apartment for Frances and me. A simple apartment, no more than two hundred dollars. I'm happy. Oh, damn it! I think I'm happy. Let me say "think." Let me not tempt the devil and bring fury and fatality onto myself. I get to the corner bodega. I grab a paper from the rack. I pay with the dollar.

"You have a pending debt," the bodega owner says. "Fifty cents."

"Me? From when?"

"A month ago. Don't you remember? A Coca-Cola."

"Oh, please! A woman as pretty as you is going to tell me that? Surely it's a mistake."

When I call her pretty, she smiles.

"I must be confused," she then says.

"That's alright."

I smile at her. I can still play a woman. It's easy. You just have to spend some time on it.

"Why don't you dye your hair blond?" I ask, still keeping up the act. "If you dyed your hair blond, you'd look so much better."

"You think so?" she says, running her fingers through her hair.

"Sure."

She opens the cash register. She puts the dollar in. She gives me back seventy-five cents.

"Thank you," I say.

"Thank *you*," she says. "The thing about the Coca-Cola must have been a mistake."

"That's alright."

I leave with the newspaper under my arm, singing *Nowhere Man* softly. A black man looks at me from the doorway of his house with sinister eyes. As I walk past, I say, "Hi, paisano!"

He smiles. "Damn, Slim. How are you? Who are you?"

"Slim," I reply. "Just Slim."

"Damn, well I'm glad to have one more friend. I'm *Clean Dough*. I arrived on a boat five years ago. I'm here for you. You've got a home here."

"Thank you," I say. "Thank you, *Clean Dough*."

"Now you know!" *Clean Dough* says, waving his fist in the air good-bye.

I continue toward the home. As I pass a house surrounded by a tall fence, an enormous black dog jumps up and starts to bark angrily. I stop. Carefully, I reach my hand over the fence and stroke his head. The dog barks one more time, confused. He sits on his hind legs and starts to lick my hand. In command of the situation, I lean over the fence and give him a kiss on the snout. I continue on my way. Upon arriving at the boarding home, I see Pedro, the silent Indian who never talks to anyone. He's sitting in the doorway of the house.

"Pedro," I say to him. "Would you like some coffee?"

"Yes," he says.

I give him a quarter.

"Thank you," he says, smiling. It's the first time I've ever seen Pedro smile.

"I'm Peruvian," he says. "From the country of the condor."

I go in. I go to the women's room and gently push the door. Frances is on her bed, drawing. I sit next to her and kiss her face. She stops drawing and takes me by the arm.

"Let's look for a house," I say.

I glance at the front page of the paper.

> *PEKING REJECTS MARX'S IDEAS AS AN-*
> *TIQUATED.*
> *AIR PIRATES ARE GOING TO KILL MORE*
> *HOSTAGES.*
> *WOMAN WHO KILLED HER HUSBAND*
> *EXONERATED.*

That's enough for me. I quickly search for the classifieds and read: "Furnished apartment. Two bedrooms. Terrace. Carpeted. Pool. Free hot water. Four hundred dollars."

"That one, my angel!" says Frances.

"No. It's very expensive."

I keep searching. I read the whole list of rentals, and, finally, point at one with my finger.

"This one."

It's on Flagler and 16th Avenue. It costs two hundred dollars. You have to go and speak with the owner in person. A woman named Haidee will see people from nine to six. It's three in the afternoon.

"I'm going there right now," I tell Frances.

"Oh my God!" she says, pressing herself against me.

"Do I look okay?" I ask her, smoothing my hair with my hands.

"I think you look okay," she says.

"Then I'm going to talk to that woman," I say.

I stand up.

"My angel," says Frances, looking for something in her drawer. "Take this and put it under your tongue when you go talk to that woman. It never fails."

"What is it?"

"A cinnamon twig," she says. "It brings good luck."

I take it and put it in my pocket.

"I'll do it," I say. I take one of her hands and kiss it. I go out to the street. As I pass by Pepe, the older of the two retards, I take his bald head in my hands and kiss it. He takes my hand.

"Do you love me, little boy?" he says.

"Of course!"

He takes one of my hands and kisses it.

"Thank you, little boy," he says, moved.

"And me? And me?" René, the other retard, asks from his chair.

"You, too," I say.

He stands up and comes over to me, dragging his feet. He hugs me tightly. Then he laughs boisterously.

"And me, William?" asks Napoleon, the Colombian midget. "Do you love me? Am I worthy of your affection?"

"Yes," I say. "You, too."

Then he comes over to me and hugs me around the waist.

"Thank you, William," he says, also moved. "Thank you for loving me, too, a sinner."

I burst out laughing. I loosen myself from his embrace. I go out to Flagler Street.

Upon arriving at Flagler and 8th Avenue, an old American in a wheelchair asks me for a cigarette. He has a blond dirty beard and is wearing rags. He's missing a leg.

I give him the cigarette.

"Sit down here, just a minute," he says, taking me by the hand.

I sit on a bench, by his side.

"Have a drink," he says, taking a bottle of plum wine out of his middle.

"No," I say. "I have to go."

"Have a drink!" he orders energetically. He takes a long swig and then passes me the bottle. I drink. I like it. I drink again.

"Are you a veteran of the Vietnam war?" I ask.

"No," he says. "I'm a veteran of the shit war."

I burst out laughing.

"Okay," I say. "But maybe you fought in the Second World War. Did you?"

"Oh, yes!" he says. "I fought in Madison Square Garden and in Disneyland, too."

All of a sudden, he becomes angry.

"Why is it you Cubans always want to see how brave I am? Go and fight your fucking mother."

"Sorry," I say.

"Don't worry," he says, calmer. "Have a drink," he takes another swig and passes me the bottle. I take three long swigs.

His face gets excited.

"You are a nice fellow," he says.

"Thank you," I say, standing up. "I have to go."

I take one of his filthy hands and squeeze tightly. A truck passes with a black American driver and a huge sign in red paint that says: "THANK YOU, BUDDY."

I let go of the American vagrant's hand and continue on my way to 16th Avenue. When I reach 12th Avenue, someone yells my name. I turn around. I barely recognize Máximo, an old friend who, like me, has been through various psychiatric clinics. He has lost a lot of weight and is wearing dirty, rag-like clothes. He's bare-foot.

"Máximo!" I say, shaking his hand. "What happened to you?"

"I chose to flee," he says. "I was in a home, like you, and chose to flee. To the streets! Anywhere!"

"Máximo," I say, "go back, damn it. You look awful."

"Don't tell me to go back!" he says, looking me in the eye, enraged. "I'll think that you're also in on the conspiracy to ruin my life."

"What conspiracy, Máximo?"

"This conspiracy!" he announces, making a

sweeping gesture with his hands. "Whores and fag-
gots!" he says. "Everyone, whore or faggot."

"Máximo . . . ," but I don't know what else to say
to him. He has chosen the street. He would rather de-
fend what is left of his freedom than live in a home with
another Curbelo, another Arsenio, another Reyes, Pepe
or René.

"It's better if you don't say anything at all to
me," he says. "Do you have money for coffee?"

I take a quarter out of my pocket and give it to
him.

"Even with all this crap," Máximo says. "Even
with all this crap, I wouldn't ever want to return to
Cuba."

I look at him. I realize that he's defending his
freedom—his freedom to wander and destroy himself
slowly. Freedom, nonetheless. I hug him. I turn on my
heels and continue on my way.

I walk several blocks until I stop, at 16th Avenue,
in front of a yellow two-story house. The number on it
corresponds to the one in the newspaper ad. The front
door is open. I go in. I look for apartment number six,
where Ms. Haidee lives. Everything smells like fresh
paint. It's pleasant. I go to door number six and ring the
bell. I wait. Inside, a dog barks. Then the door opens
and a fat woman, about fifty years old, appears.

"Haidee?" I say. "I've come about the newspaper ad."

"Come in," she says pleasantly.

I go in. I sit on a sofa. She sits in front of me in a wicker chair. She examines my face.

"Aren't you from Havana?"

"Yes."

"Didn't your family live on San Rafael street, near the Rex Cinema?"

"Yes," I say, surprised.

"Aren't you the son of Dr. Figueras, the lawyer whose office was near the Capitol building?"

"That's right."

"Isn't your mom's name Carmela?"

"Yes," I exclaim, laughing.

"Kid!" she says happily. "I was your mother's friend for many years. We used to sell Avon products together."

"How amazing!" I say.

"Are you here about the apartment?" "Yes," I say. "There are two of us. My wife and me."

"Do you want to see it?"

"Yes."

She gets up from her chair and goes over to a sideboard. She opens a drawer and takes out a bunch of keys. She smiles the whole time.

"How lucky that you were the one to come!" she says. "I don't like renting to strangers."

We leave. We walk down a dark hallway and stop in front of a door marked with a number two. Haidee opens the door. We go in.

"It's magnificent!" I think upon entering.

The apartment is freshly painted. Roomy and well-lit. The kitchen is new. So is the refrigerator. There's a full-size bed, three armchairs and a sideboard.

"Closet . . . ," she says, opening a large closet.

"I like it," I say, excited. "I'll take it."

"Right now?" Haidee asks.

"No, tomorrow. Can you hold it for me until tomorrow?"

She smiles.

"I can," she says. "I don't normally do that, but for you, I'll hold it."

"Thank you, Haidee . . ."

"Your mother and I were great friends," she says: "Great!"

She takes me by the arm.

"You won't have any troubles here," she says. "Everyone is very peaceful. The market is close by. And besides, I'll be here."

"Is electricity free, Haidee?"

"Electricity and gas," she says. "You get everything for two hundred. But this month you have to pay one hundred dollars extra. The owner's request," she explains. "If it were up to me, you wouldn't have to pay anything."

"I know," I say.

We talk a little while longer. About Havana, about friends in common, about her plan to travel to Cuba in the coming months. We talk about Madrid, a place where we both spent time before arriving in the United States. At last, I shake her hand.

"Okay, Haidee, expect me tomorrow afternoon," I tell her.

She brings me close to her and kisses my cheek.

"I'm so glad to have you as a neighbor!" she says. "You'll be fine here."

I kiss her face.

"Goodbye, Haidee," I say, backing away toward the front door.

"See you tomorrow," she says, waving from the door.

I go back out onto the street. The sun is setting. I stop on the sidewalk for a few moments and take a deep breath. I smile. I'd like to have Frances with me right now and hug her tightly. Slowly, leisurely. I go back to the halfway house.

I get to the halfway house around six in the evening. Mr. Curbelo has left and at his desk sits Arsenio, who's in charge, with his ever-present can of Budweiser in hand.

"Hey, Mafia," he says when he sees me come in. "Sit down a while here. Let's talk."

I sit in a chair by him. I look at his face. Although I find him intensely repulsive, I feel a little pity. He's only thirty-two-years old and the only thing he knows how to do is drink beer and play numbers. His dream is to win a thousand dollars all at once and then . . .

"If I win, Mafia, if number 38 comes out to-night, I'll buy a truck and start a business picking up old boxes. Do you know how much they pay for a ton of cardboard? Seventy dollars! Do you want to work with me on that truck?"

"First, number 38 has to win," I say. "Then, I'm sure you'll drink the thousand dollars in one day."

He bursts out laughing.

"I would stop drinking," he says. "I swear I would stop drinking."

"You're already lost," I say. "You're an animal, my dear friend."

"Why?" he says. "Why don't you respect me, Mafia? Why doesn't anyone love me?"

"Your life is a mess," I say. "You've settled in here, in this filthy house. If you need two bucks, you steal from the nuts. If you feel like being with a woman, you screw Hilda, that decrepit old hag. Curbelo exploits you, but you're happy. You beat the nuts up. You give orders like a drill sergeant. You lack creativity."

He laughs again.

"One day I'll crown!" he says.

"What do you mean by 'crown'?" I say.

"Crown means, in old criminal speak, you make a major hit. Steal something big. One hundred thousand. Two hundred thousand. Here, as you look at me,

I'm planning a big hit. And I'll crown. I'll crown! And then I'll say to you, 'Here, Mafia, have two hundred dollars. Do you need more? Take three hundred!'"

"You're a dreamer," I say. "Drink. It's the best you can do."

"You'll see!" he says. "You'll see me around Miami—twenty gold chains around my neck with a hot blonde at my side! You'll see me in a Cadillac Dorado! You'll see me with a three-thousand-dollar watch and a six-hundred-dollar suit. You'll see me, Mafia!"

"I hope you crown!" I say.

"You'll see me."

I stand up, I make a half turn and walk toward the women's room. When I get there, I softly nudge the door and go inside. Frances is on her bed, putting her clothes in two paper bags. I go over to her and hug her gently around the waist. I kiss her neck.

"My angel!" she says. "Did you see that woman? Did you get the house?"

"Yes," I say. "Tomorrow at this time, we'll be sleeping in a clean delicious bed."

"Oh, my God!" she says, looking up at the ceiling. "Oh, my God!"

"A dining room." I say. "One bedroom. A kitchen. A bathroom. All of it clean, pretty, freshly painted. All for us."

"My angel, my angel!" she says. "Kiss me!"

I kiss her on the mouth. I squeeze one of her breasts through her dress. She smells good. If she weighed a few more pounds and took better care of herself, she'd be pretty. I lay her down gently on the bed. I remove her shoes. I go to the door and lock it. She takes her own clothes off this time.

"Tomorrow . . . ," I say as I enter her slowly. "Tomorrow we'll be doing this in our own house."

"My angel . . . ," she says.

I dreamt that I was in Havana again, in a funeral parlor on Calle 23. I was surrounded by numerous friends. We were drinking coffee. All of a sudden, a white door opened and in came a casket on the shoulders of a dozen wailing women. One of my friends elbowed me in the ribs and said, "They're bringing in Fidel Castro."

We turned around. The old ladies placed the coffin in the middle of the room and left, weeping hysterically. Then the coffin opened. Fidel stuck a hand out first. Then the top half of his body. Finally all of him emerged. He smoothed his full-dress uniform and approached us, a smile on his face.

"Isn't there any coffee for me?" he asked.

Somebody gave him a cup.

"Well, we're already dead," Fidel said. "Now you'll see that doesn't solve anything, either."

I wake up. It's morning already. It's the big day. In three hours the social security checks will arrive and Frances and I will leave the halfway house. I jump out of bed. I grab the filthy towel and a sliver of soap and head for the bathroom. I wash up. I urinate. I leave the towel and the soap in the bathroom knowing that I won't need them anymore. I head for the living room. The nuts are having breakfast, but Frances is there, sitting in a corner next to the TV.

"I couldn't sleep," she says. "Let's leave now!"

"We have to wait," I say. "The checks are coming at ten."

"I'm scared," she says. "Let's leave now!"

"Calm down," I say. "Calm down. Did you already get your things together?"

"Yes."

"Then calm down," I say, kissing the top of her head.

I look at her. Just thinking that this afternoon I will be making love to her in a clean soft bed makes me hard.

"Calm down," I say, sticking my hand down her dress and gently squeezing a breast. "Calm down."

I let go. I stick my hand in my pockets and find that I have two quarters left. Great. I'll drink some coffee. I'll buy a newspaper and I'll spend the next two hours, until the checks arrive, sitting on some bench. I kiss her on the mouth. I head out to the corner diner.

It's a beautiful morning. For the first time in a long time I look at the blue sky, the birds, the clouds. Drinking coffee—lighting up a cigarette—flipping through today's newspaper: all suddenly become delicious things to do. For the first time in a long time I feel the weight is falling off my shoulders. Like my legs can run. Like my arms could test their strength. I take a rock from the street and throw it a long way, toward a barren field. I remember that when I was a kid, I was a good baseball player. I stop. I inhale the morning's fresh air. My eyes fill with tears of happiness. I get to the diner and order coffee.

"Make it good," I tell the woman.

The woman makes it with a smile on her face.

"Special, for you," she says, filling the cup.

I drink it in three sips. It's good. I ask for a newspaper, too. The woman brings it. I pay. I turn around, looking for a clean quiet spot. My eyes settle on a white wall, by the shade of a tree. I go and sit there. I open the newspaper and start to read. A feeling of peace washes over me.

> *SPURNED EX-BOYFRIEND KIDNAPS, GAGS AND KILLS HER.*
> *DEATH THREATENS DARING HELICOPTER PILOTS IN THE DARK.*
> *RUSSIAN LEADER PROPOSES A FAREWELL TO ARMS.*

Someone stands over me. I raise my head. It's Frances. She followed me. She sits next to me. She takes me by the arm. She buries her head in my chest and stays still for a few seconds.

"The mailman arrived," she murmurs finally.

"Do you know if he brought the checks?"

"I don't know," she says. "That man . . . Curbelo, he grabbed the envelopes."

"Let's go!" I say.

I leave the newspaper on the wall and stand up. I lift her gently by the arm. She's shaking.

Looking up at the sky, she says, "Oh, my God!"

"Calm down . . . ," I'm dragging her gently.

"Is the house beautiful, my angel?"

"It's perfect," I say, squeezing her shoulders. "It has a living and dining room, a bedroom, a kitchen, a bathroom, a full-size bed, a sideboard, three chairs . . ."

We walk toward the halfway house.

When we get to the home, she goes to her room to pick up the last of her belongings and I go to my room to get my suitcase. When I pass Curbelo's desk, I see that, sure enough, he's there opening the envelopes with the social security checks. One-eyed Reyes goes up to him and asks for a cigarette.

"Get away!" Curbelo says. "Can't you see that I'm working?"

I smile. I go on to my room. I grab the suitcase and stick two or three shirts in it, my books, a jacket and a pair of shoes. I close it. My books, more than fifty of them, make it pretty heavy. I take out the book of English Romantic poets and stick it in my pocket. I take one last look at the room. The crazy guy who works at the pizzeria is snoring in his bed with his mouth agape. A small cockroach runs across his face. I leave. I let my suitcase drop in front of Mr. Curbelo's desk. He looks at me questioningly.

"Give me my check," I say. "I'm leaving."

"That's not the way things are done around here," he says. "I'll give it to you, but that's not the way things are done. You should have given me fifteen days' notice. Now you're leaving me with an empty bed. That's money that I lose."

"I'm sorry," I say. "Give me my check."

He looks for it in the collection of envelopes. He takes it out and gives it to me.

"Get out of here!" he says, irritated.

I leave. I place the suitcase in one corner of the living room, and go to the women's room. Frances is there with her bags ready. I show her my check.

"Go and ask for yours," I say.

She goes out in search of Curbelo. I sit on her bed and wait. After an interminably long time, she reappears with her face pale and her hands empty.

"He doesn't want to give it to me," she says.

"Why not?" I ask, furious.

I run to Curbelo's desk.

"Frances's check," I say, standing before him. "She's leaving with me."

"That's not possible," Curbelo says, looking over his glasses at me.

"Why not?"

"Because Frances is a sick woman," he says. "Her mother brought Frances to this establishment herself and left her in my care. I am responsible for whatever happens to her."

"Responsible!" I cry scornfully. "Responsible for dirty sheets and filthy towels. For puddles of piss and inedible food."

"That's a lie!" he says. "This is a tightly run operation."

Indignant, I take a step toward him and snatch the stack of checks out of his hands. He stands up. He tries to take them away from me, but I give him a shove that makes him fall on his ass in the wastebasket.

"Arsenio!" he yells from there. "Arsenio!"

I quickly look for Frances's check. I find it. I put it in my pocket and throw the rest of the envelopes on the desk. Frances is waiting for me at the door.

"Go!" I yell.

She walks out with her two enormous bags. I walk out behind her with my heavy suitcase.

"My angel . . . ," Frances says.

"Walk!" I say. "We have to get away from here!"

"But this is so heavy," she says, pointing at her bags.

I pull one of the bags out of her hands and carry it, along with my suitcase.

"Arsenio!" Curbelo yells from inside.

We walk quickly down First Street toward Six-teenth Avenue. But my suitcase is enormous and old, and as we reach Seventh Avenue it pops wide open, scatter-ing books and clothing all over the ground. I bend down quickly to pick up the books. I shove a few back in the suitcase. A police siren wails, then a patrol car stops in front of us, blocking our way. I stand up slowly. Curbelo and a policeman get out of the car.

"All right, paisano . . . ," the policeman says, tak-ing me by the arm. "Stay still, paisano. Is this the pai-sano?" the policeman asks Curbelo.

"Yes," he says.

"All right, paisano," the policeman says in an even-tempered, almost indifferent voice.

"Give me those checks."

"They're ours!" I say.

Then Curbelo says, "He's crazy. He's out of whack. He doesn't take his pills."

"Give them to me, paisano," the policeman says.

I don't have to give them to him. He notices that I have them in my shirt pocket and grabs them.

"He's a very problematic kid," Curbelo says.

I look at Frances. She's crying. She's bent down on the ground, still picking up my scattered books. She looks at Curbelo with rage and throws a book at his face. The policeman takes me by the arm and leads me to the car. He opens the back door and tells me to get inside. I get in. He closes the door. He goes back to where Cur-belo is. They whisper to each other for a few minutes.

Then I see Curbelo lift Frances up from the ground and pick up one of her bags. Then he takes her by the arm and starts to drag her back to the halfway house.

The policeman picks my things up from the ground and tosses them any which way in the trunk of the patrol car. Then he gets in the car and sits at the wheel.

"I'm sorry, paisano," he says, starting the engine.

The car takes off quickly.

The patrol car crossed all of Miami and entered the northern neighborhoods. Finally it stopped in front of a large gray building. The policeman got out of the car and opened the back door.

"Get out," he ordered.

I got out. He took me forcefully by the arm and led me to some sort of large, well-lit lobby. We stopped before a small office that said "Admissions." The policeman pushed my shoulders and we entered the office.

"Sit," he ordered.

I sat on a bench. Then the policeman went up to a desk and spoke in a low voice to a young woman wearing a long white coat.

"Paisano," the policeman then said, turning toward me, "come here!"

I walk over to him.

"You're in a hospital," he tells me, "You'll stay here until you're cured. Got it?"

"There's nothing wrong with me," I say. "I just want to go live somewhere decent with my girlfriend."

"That," the policeman says, "is something you have to explain to the doctors later." He slaps his holster. He smiles at the woman behind the desk. He leaves the office slowly. The woman gets up, grabs a pile of keys from the drawer and says to me, "Come with me."

I follow her. She opens a huge door with one of the keys and leads me into a dirty, poorly lit room. There's a man with a long gray beard who is nearly naked. He recites fragments from Nietzsche's *Zarathustra* in a loud voice. There are also several ragged-looking black men sharing a cigarette in silence. I also see a white guy sobbing softly in a corner and crying, "Mama, where are you?" There's a black woman with a decent figure who gazes at me with a drugged look, and a white woman who seems like a prostitute, with huge breasts that fall down to her navel. It's already nighttime. I walk down a long hallway leading to a room full of iron beds. In a corner, I see a public telephone. I take a quarter out of my pocket and insert it. I dial the number of the halfway house. I wait. Arsenio answers on the third ring.

"Mafia?" he says to me. "Is that you?"

"It's me," I say. "Get Frances on the line."

"She's in her room," Arsenio says. "Curbelo injected her with two doses of chlorpromazine and put her to bed. She was screaming. She didn't want to eat. She tore her dress in half with her own hands. Mafia . . . what did you do to that woman? She's crazy about you."

"Never mind," I say. "I'll call again tomorrow."

"Your books are here." Arsenio says. "The policeman brought them. Mafia, I'm telling you this man to man, you know why you went nuts? From reading."

"Never mind," I say. "Keep hoping number 38 comes up."

"Sure thing," says Arsenio. "You'll see me around Miami. You'll see me!"

"Talk to you later," I say.

"Later," Arsenio says.

As soon as I hang up, from the main hall I hear someone yelling my name. I go there. A man in a white coat is waiting for me.

"Are you William Figueras?"

"I am."

"Come inside. I want to talk to you. I am Dr. Paredes."

I walk into a small windowless office. There's a desk and three chairs. The walls are decorated with pictures of the writer Ernest Hemingway.

"Are you a fan of Hemingway?" I ask, taking a seat.

"I've read him," Dr. Paredes says. "A lot."

"Have you read *Islands in the Stream*?"

"Yes," he says. "Have you read *Death in the Afternoon*?"

"No," I say, "but I read *A Moveable Feast*."

"Excellent," the doctor says. "Maybe now we'll understand each other better. All right, William, what happened to you?"

"I wanted to be free again," I say. "I wanted to escape the home where I was living and start a new life."

"You took a girl with you?"

"Yes," I say. "Frances, my future wife. She was coming with me."

"The policeman said you were abducting her."

"The policeman is lying," I say. "He's just repeating what he heard from Mr. Curbelo, the owner of the home. That woman and I love each other."

"Love love?" Dr. Paredes asks.

"Love," I say. "Maybe it wasn't a great love yet. But it was blossoming."

"Do you hear voices, William?"

"I used to," I say. "I don't hear them anymore."

"Do you have visions?"

"I used to. I don't see them anymore."

"What cured you?"

"Frances," I say. "Having her by my side made me a new man."

"If what you're saying is true, I'll help you." Dr. Paredes says. "You'll spend a few days here and I will personally try to fix this problem. I'll talk to Curbelo."

"Do you know him?"

"Yes."

"What do you think of him?"

"He's a businessman. Nothing more than a businessman."

"Exactly," I say. "And a son of a bitch, besides."

"Okay," Dr. Paredes says to me, "now you can go. We'll speak again tomorrow."

"Do you have a cigarette?"

"Yes," he says. "Keep the pack."

He hands me a full pack of Winstons. I pocket it. I leave the office. I go back to the room with the other nuts. I arrive at the exact moment that the man who was reciting Zarathustra has trapped a black woman in a corner and has begun to lift her dress forcefully. The woman tries to slap him away. The Zarathustra guy throws the woman to the floor and starts to touch her thighs and her sex. While he's doing it, he says with a voice from beyond the grave:

> I have walked through valleys and mountains.
> And I have had the world at my feet.
> O man who atoneth: suffer!
> O man believeth: have faith!
> O rebellious man: attack and kill!

I leave and head toward the room with the iron beds. I get to one of these beds and let myself fall on it. I think of Frances. I remember her next to me, in the entryway of that Baptist church, her shoulder pressing into my ribs.

"My angel . . . were you ever a communist?"

"Yes."

"Me too. In the beginning. In the beginning. In the beginning . . ."

I fall asleep. I dream that Frances and I run away at full speed through a field of vegetables. All of a sudden, we see headlights in the distance. It's Curbelo's car. We drop to the ground so he won't see us. Curbelo drives the car through the sown vegetables. He stops next to us. He pretends not to see us. Frances and I are holding hands, almost melting into the earth. Curbelo gets out of the car with his large speargun. He stands over me with his frog legs.

"Two sturgeons!" he yells loudly. "Two huge sturgeons! This time I'll definitely win first place! The gold cup will be mine! Mine!"

Frances and I bite the dirt beneath his feet.

I spent seven days at the state hospital. I called the half-way house one more time, but Arsenio answered again with the news that Frances remained unconscious in her bed. I couldn't call anymore. I ran out of change. I also ran out of cigarettes.

On the seventh day, Dr. Paredes called me into his office again.

"I have something," he says.

He takes out a poster of Hemingway and gives it to me.

"Is it a gift?"

"Yes, so you have a little faith in life."

"Okay," I say. "What wall will I hang it on?"

"Don't worry," he says. "Maybe you can hang it in that clean, well-lighted room where you wanted to move."

"Will Frances come too?"

"We'll have to see about that," he says. "Now you and I are going to talk to Mr. Curbelo. If the girl wants to go with you, no one can prevent her."

"I'm glad," I say.

"This is a free country," Paredes says.

"I believe you," I say.

I look at the Hemingway poster. It's a sad Hemingway. I tell Paredes this.

"He was already a sick man," he says. "That was one of the last photos they took of him before he died."

"He wanted to be a god," I say.

"And he almost got there," says Paredes.

He stands up. He goes over to the office door and opens it.

"Let's go," he says. "Let's go to the halfway house."

I walk out after him. We walk together down the long hallway. Paredes stops in front of the large entry door and opens it with his key.

"Let's go," he says.

We go out to the lobby, cross it, and walk toward the hospital parking lot.

"I'm doing this for you," Paredes says. "I don't think I've ever done this for anyone."

"Oh, let's go!" I say. "Have you read *The Short Happy Life of Frances McComber*?"

"Yes. It's very good. Have you read *The Mother of an Ace*?"

"I don't like it as much. I prefer *The Revolutionary*."

"I'm doing this for you," Paredes laughs. "Because in this damned city, I don't think anyone has read Hemingway the way you have."

We get to a small car. Paredes opens the passenger door. I get in.

"I wanted to be a writer," Paredes says, turning on the car. "I'd still like to be one!"

We head toward the boarding home. On the way, Paredes takes a typed sheet of paper out of the glove compartment and hands it to me.

"I wrote this yesterday," he says. "Let's see what you think of it."

It's a vignette. It's about an old butler who has spent fifty years in a man's service. When the man dies, the butler goes up to the cadaver, contemplates it silently for a long time and spits in its face. Then he cleans the spit, covers the dead man's face with a sheet again, and leaves, dragging his feet.

"It's very good," I say.

"I'm glad you like it," he says.

We cross the city, heading west. We get to Flagler Street again and turn left, toward downtown. A few more blocks and we're there.

"Does Curbelo know we're coming?" I ask the doctor.

"Yes. He's waiting for us."

We get out of the car. Right away, all of the nuts who were sitting on the porch's wooden chairs descend upon us, asking for cigarettes. Paredes takes out a pack of Winstons and gives it to them. We go inside. Curbelo is seated at his desk.

"Oh, my!" Curbelo says to Dr. Paredes: "Long time, no see!"

They shake hands. Paredes and I sit in front of Curbelo's desk.

"How are those fishing competitions going?" Paredes asks.

"Well!" Curbelo says. "Yesterday, I won first place. The first time in twenty years that I win first place!"

"Congratulations!" Paredes says. Then he turns to me and asks, "William . . . can you leave us alone for a minute?"

I get up and leave. I go to my room. The crazy guy who works at the pizza place jumps up from his bed when he sees me.

"Mister William!" he exclaims happily. "We thought you were in prison!"

Ida, Pepe, René, Eddy, all of the nuts have come to my room and start to greet me effusively.

"Are you here to stay, Mister William?"

"No," I say. "I'm leaving with Frances to go to our own house."

Then Ida, the grande dame come to ruin, comes up to me and puts her hands on my shoulders.

"Take it easy," she says.

"What?"

"About Frances," she says. "Take it easy!"

"What happened?"

"Frances isn't here anymore," Ida says. "Yesterday, her mother came from New Jersey and took her."

I don't listen to anything else. I push Ida on the bed and run to the women's room. I open the door violently. Instead of Frances, I see a fat, old black woman lying on her bed.

"I arrived yesterday," the woman says. "The one who was here before left."

"Did she leave a note?" I ask, anxiously.

"No," says the woman. "She only left this."

And she shows me Frances' drawings. There we all are. There's Caridad, the *mulata* cook. There's one-eyed Reyes; there's Eddy, the nut who is well-versed in international politics; there's Arsenio, with his devilish eyes; and there I am, with my face that is hardened and sad at the same time.

I go up to Mr. Curbelo's desk. Paredes looks at me questioningly.

"You know everything already?"

"I already know," I respond. "Don't bother yourself about me anymore. Nothing can be done."

"I'm sorry," Paredes says.

"Kid . . . ," Mr. Curbelo says. "You can stay here if you want. Take your pills. Rest. There are enough women in this world."

From the dining room comes the *mulata* Caridad's voice announcing dinner. The nuts pile out in droves. Curbelo stands up and pushes me gently by the shoulders.

"Go," he says. "Eat. You won't do better anywhere else in the world than here."

I hang my head. I go toward the dining room, behind all the nuts.

Boarding home! Boarding home! I've been living in this halfway house for three years already. Castaño, the old centenarian who always wants to die, is still screaming and reeking of urine. Ida, the grande dame come to ruin, is still dreaming that her kids in Massachusetts will come to her rescue one day. Eddy, the nut who is well-versed in international politics, still follows the TV news avidly and screams for a third world war. Old one-eyed Reyes is still oozing pus from his glass eye. Arsenio is still bossing everyone around. Curbelo goes on living his bourgeois life with the money he takes from us.

Boarding home! Boarding home!

GUILLERMO ROSALES

I open the book of English poets and read a poem by Blake called "Proverbs of Hell":

> *Drive your cart and plow over the bones of the dead.*
> *The road of excess leads to the palace of wisdom.*
> *He who desires but acts not, breeds pestilence.*
> *The hours of folly are measur'd by the clock*

I stand up. In a corner of the living room, one-eyed Reyes is taking a long piss. Arsenio goes over to him and takes off his belt. With the buckle, he whips the old one-eyed man's back violently. I go over to Arsenio and take the belt out of his hands. I lift it up over my head and let it fall down with all my might on the old one-eyed man's frail body.

Outside, Caridad the *mulata* calls us to eat. There's cold fish, white rice and raw lentils.